THE EMPEROR'S SERVANT

THE
EMPEROR'S SERVANT

Four Tales of the Napoleonic Wars

by

DAVID PILGRIM

LONDON
MACMILLAN & CO. LTD
1946

Preface

Two of these tales, " The Stolen General " and " The Poodle of the Princess Alberoni ", appeared in the *Cornhill*. The courtesy of its Editor in consenting to their publication is gratefully acknowledged.

Contents

JOHN PALMER
1885–1944

A MEMOIR, BY HILARY ST. GEORGE SAUNDERS

> His life was gentle, and the elements
> So mix'd in him that Nature might stand up
> And say to all the world, " This was a man ! "

THE rain poured down. John Palmer and I were new to the mountains of Savoy. We had two days' leave, and though we had been in Geneva for some months we had not yet caught even a glimpse of Mont Blanc.

That May day of 1921 — it was the Feast of the Ascension, I recall, and why the infant Secretariat of the League of Nations had been given a holiday we neither knew nor cared — we had set our faces to the mountains for the first time. They were there somewhere behind the curtain of warm, misty rain, and we were determined to reach them whatever the weather.

Yet, as we boarded the tram-car in the Cours de Rive — the only street name in Geneva that John could ever remember — our spirits were nearly as damp as our clothes. It seemed a day on which even Noah would have felt depressed, and he at least had known what was coming and had doubtless had the satisfaction of watching all the persons that he especially disliked perish in a fashion at once gratifying and comprehensive.

The tram-car was a well-appointed vehicle of undecided habits, for it moved now forwards, now backwards, as if hesitating to venture too far from the depot, till anon a voice outside cried, " Attention to the grand manœuvre ! " So might Tilly or Napoleon have addressed their staffs when about to join battle with Mansfeld or Bagration.

We lurched again and then clattered forward through the inexorable downpour till we reached Moille-Sulaz and the French frontier. Here we abandoned the Swiss tram for a French coach belonging to the " Economical Iron Road of the North ", and in it eventually reached the little mountain town of Samoëns.

We arrived at dusk, a rainy, friendly dusk which yielded only with the greatest deliberation to a sullenly determined night. During the prolonged surrender we dined, drinking with our meal, if I remember, a bottle of Pommard of the 1915 vintage, a trifle young in those days — it was, I repeat, May 1921 — but a fine, robust wine, the proper drink for a wet evening.

After dinner, desirous of stretching our legs before going to bed, we left the inn and found ourselves crossing the village square. It was then that we heard the music. John stopped abruptly and turned his head. The tune, drifting on the night air, was simple and repetitive, and seemed to come from twenty feet up in the black night. It was accompanied by a prolonged rumbling sound.

" An avalanche," I said.

" An avalanche to music ? " John's tone was doubtful.

" It is the gods of the mountain," I went on, " walking to music." (I had met W. B. Yeats at Oxford two years before and was still under the spell of his Celtic twilight.)

" Well, they've hired a very poor orchestra," rejoined John briskly. " The fiddle's half a tone flat," and he stepped out towards the sound.

I followed, and soon we were at the foot of an outside staircase climbing the blank wall of a building considerably larger than any we had yet seen. We groped our way upwards in the thick darkness till a sword of light beneath a door shone on our heavy, mud-stained mountain boots. John pushed it open, and the tune and its accompaniment smote us like thunder. Then it ceased abruptly as though cut off by our entry.

We found ourselves in an upper chamber with a row of chairs along two of its walls. There was a small dais at the far end, on which sat three aged men clasping instruments of music I have never seen before or since. Moving towards the chairs were what appeared to be all the female population of Samoëns, arrayed in black skirts and many-coloured blouses. On the other side of the room the men of the town were congregated several deep in front of a trestle table on which stood carafes of pale white wine and thick-rimmed tumblers. At the end of the hall, above the heads of the musicians, was a yellow banner with the words " Les Young Boys " embroidered on it in black.

It took us a few moments, and an entrance fee of two francs each, to discover that we had gate-crashed the annual ball of the local football club, but, as soon as they knew us to be English, almost in no time they invited us to join the dance. The three musicians struck up a tune. We clasped the partners provided for us by Monsieur le Maire, and with the courage of ignorance set forth.

It was at this point that disaster overwhelmed John Palmer.

" It is necessary to be circumspect," murmured my partner, who held my left hand firmly and advanced, not backwards in front of me, but by my side.

I soon saw what she meant. There were perhaps twice as many dancers as the room would comfortably hold. The measure we were treading was something like an old-fashioned barn dance, two steps forward, three steps back, then twirl your partner. All was well, provided these grand manœuvres were carried out simultaneously and with percision by all concerned.

They were, with one unhappy exception. John moved backwards when he should have moved forwards. His collision with the Mayor immediately behind was cataclysmic. It was as though a steam-roller had struck him, and he crashed to the ground. But the motto of The Young Boys was evidently " On with the Dance ", for, before his partner could disentangle him from the moving forest of stout legs, three couples had trampled him in the dust. He was pulled out at last, clutching his pince-nez — it was before the days when he wore horn-rimmed spectacles — a trifle part-worn, but still sound in wind and limb. The dance was stopped. Apologies poured as fast as the pale wine, while a small boy went round the room laying the dust with lustral water sprinkled from open palms.

" The Young Boys," I said, by way of making conversation and with a glance at the banner above the orchestra, " have doubtless scored a great victory and you are celebrating it, Monsieur le Maire ? "

The Mayor shook his head.

" The season has not yet begun," he said, " but we hope to have many, for this time we shall have a ball. Your entrance has made up the exact sum required, and Clement here will go to Annecy to buy it."

At the time of this incident, I had known John for some six months. We first met in a panelled room in the West End of London, when I was a young undergraduate seeking a temporary job to arrest the havoc wrought in my finances by a year and a half at Oxford. My tutor, the great H. W. C. Davis, had been a colleague of John during the First German War, when they had worked together in the War Trade Intelligence Department of the Foreign Office — John's very defective eyesight had made it impossible for him to join the Services — and Davis had a very high opinion of him.

" He came to Balliol," he told me, " from King Edward's School, as a Brackenbury History Scholar with a brilliant record behind him. He is very good with his pen, and if ever you want to write you cannot do better than work with John Palmer."

The words were prophetic, though as I climbed the dusty stairs, up and down which flitted wan, distracted females trying to cope with the grim task of moving the seat of the League of Nations from London to Geneva, I had no thought that in twenty years we should write forty books together.

I presently found myself face to face with him, a short man seated at a large desk with a telephone at his ear. " No, don't send the spoons with the heavy luggage," he was saying. Presently he turned a pair of dark and singularly observant eyes upon me, and in five minutes I found myself engaged as his temporary assistant for a period of two months.

That temporary job lasted seventeen years, and it was during that period that our friendship and literary partnership grew and flourished. The first was formed very quickly, the second grew out of it. We had known each other for not quite three years when we decided to write " thrillers " together.

We did so for a good and imperative reason. Geneva was very expensive and we both wanted to increase our incomes. It was my suggestion, and I made it one winter day walking across the Pont du Mont Blanc in a howling north-easterly wind, the famous *bise*, which in winter can turn Geneva into an Arctic city in an hour. Though by that time we were firm friends and had few secrets from each other, I made the proposal with some diffidence.

Apart from a short story published in an ephemeral undergraduate quarterly called the *Oxford Outlook*, one or two bad poems in the *Isis*, and two weekly columns of journalcsc in the *Oxford Chronicle*, I had written nothing. John Palmer, on the other hand, had been a distinguished literary figure for many years. Already the author of two novels, he was to write five more, of which *Jennifer*, a story in the manner of Pirandello, and *The Hesperides*, a vivid and original incursion into the field of Erewhon, were the most remarkable.

But it was not so much his literary distinction which made our partnership so sure and certain a source of happiness to me, and I hope for him, for more than twenty years. It was John's entire inability to feel remarkable. His was an instructive and wise humility which made it not merely an honour, but a delight to work with him. From the first moment, he treated me as a full and equal partner in the enterprise, though at the beginning at least the drafts of each chapter which I presented to him — every book was written chapter by chapter twice, once by me and then by John who used my text as an incentive or corrective — were so crude that he had to rewrite nine-tenths of them. Never by word or look or gesture did he suggest that they were crude or that I was in any way so clearly his inferior in the difficult and glorious art of writing. Nor did he ever look upon our undertaking as so much wood-chopping to boil the pot. From first to last we were equal, sharing the labour and the reward. I would supply the general plot and the " mechanics " of the story (what the heroine wore, what train, aircraft, bicycle or fleet-footed steed the hero took to reach her side, what weapons the villain or villains preferred and why), he the characters and the dialogue, while both of us argued happily about the detailed plot.

For the historical novels we wrote together under the

pseudonym of David Pilgrim, we used much the same technique. Writing them was a delight to both of us ; John, I fancy, because he was a fine historian eager not to let his love and knowledge of history rust, and I because I had by then learnt from him something of the art and craft of writing. The last specimens of David Pilgrim's work follow this memoir. They consist of four tales of the Napoleonic Wars, two of them, " The Stolen General " and " The Poodle of the Princess Alberoni ", published by the courtesy of the *Cornhill*. Had John lived, we had hoped to write several more, for we were both of us fascinated by Napoleon.

On leaving Oxford in 1909, John became private secretary to the Honourable Gervase Beckett, at that time Member of Parliament for Whitby. Beckett was a man of the world and John, young, eager and gifted with a shrewd tongue and an itching pen, learnt much of men and affairs. After three years spent in close contact with Parliamentary circles — years which, as he more than once told me, taught him both what to observe and how to observe it — he married, his wife being Mildred Hodson-Woodfield. The connection with Beckett continued but its nature changed, for Beckett, owner of the *Saturday Review*, made John a member of its editorial staff. The paper could boast of famous contributors, Max Beerbohm and Bernard Shaw among them ; their views on music or on the theatre had amused and instructed the public for a number of years, but their successor, the young man from Balliol, was not dismayed. He had views of his own and he knew that he possessed the power to express them.

Soon his dramatic notices began to attract attention. Some of it was hostile, especially when the field of his activities had widened and he was writing on the theatre for the *Evening Standard*, but all of it was interesting, and his name soon became more widely known by the publication in quick succession of an essay on Comedy, an essay on George Bernard Shaw and a pamphlet on that evergreen subject, the Censor and the Theatre.

The essay on Comedy marked out John as a writer of distinction — it has become a text-book for all serious students of the drama — but his reputation was made by his next book, *The Comedy of Manners*, a study of the comic dramatists of the Restoration. It earned him " high commendation, true applause " and, what he valued very greatly, the distinction of a cartoon by Max Beerbohm. In it John is portrayed surrounded by the affable forms of Congreve, Wycherley, Etheridge and others, who are larding him with seventeenth-century compliments on the soundness of his defence of their attitude to life and on the temerity with which he had presented it.

John Palmer was now an established critic, destined, it seemed certain, to an honourable career in a profession which, though lately stigmatised by a dreary intellectual as attracting " morbid parasites . . . vampires . . . and monstrosities ", has numbered among its ranks William Hazlitt and Charles Lamb.

But the First German War broke out and for John, as for many more, the bright future became obscured. There followed four years of drudgery in a Government office, punctuated by desperate attempts to join up — on account of his bad eyesight no doctor would look at him — and lightened by the births of his son and daughter.

Then in 1919, when he was serving with the British Delegation to the Paris Peace Conference, came an offer which, though it meant the end of dramatic criticism, would, if accepted, make it possible for John to share in the conduct of a new experiment in international relations. The Permanent Secretariat of the League of Nations was being formed, and, filled with enthusiasm for what he knew was a just and what he hoped would be a successful cause, John joined its ranks. By September of that year he was installed as Head of the English Précis-Writing Service, destined, though he did not yet know it, to do almost everything but write précis, and it was a year later when we met for the first time.

By then John was beginning to have doubts, but he did not express them to me until soon after the first Assembly, when I asked him whether, in his opinion, I should continue to work for the League. An opportunity to do so for several years, and possibly indefinitely, had arisen, and I wanted his advice.

To my surprise he urged me to return to Oxford. We argued the matter at length during a long walk up a local mountain, the Salève, a favourite place with John, where we afterwards plotted a novel on Napoleon. " This scheme," he said in effect, " is an illusion. At the first real test it broke down," and he went on to describe a scene which had taken place a year before at one of the very early meetings of the League Council. On that occasion Poland was brought to task for allowing Zeligowski, " that ambiguous General with his forces of uncertain allegiance ", as Balfour afterwards described him, to occupy the Lithuanian town of Vilna. The Council decided against Poland, whereupon her Prime Minister, the great pianist, Paderewski, rose, walked round the table and held out his hand to the Lithuanian representative, saying that, since this was the judgement of the world's supreme authority, he must accept it.

" We were all somewhat overcome," continued John, " and everyone looked at each other with a wild surmise, for it seemed that the new machinery was going to work and that the Council had only to decree to be obeyed."

He paused, and then added : " The next day Paderewski was out, disowned by his Government, and the Polish-Lithuanian dispute is still on the agenda ".

I would not agree with him that day, and it was not until two years later, when a timid Council and an impotent Assembly allowed Mussolini to shell Corfu and to kill refugees for whom the League was responsible, that I realised how accurate an estimate John had made of its capacities. By then it was too late for us to leave, or at least for John, with a growing family, the risk was too great. Nor, with the spectacle before me of so many of my friends in England without jobs, had I the courage to abandon the amenities of Geneva for the uncertainties of London. So I stayed, and watched with John the decline of an institution which failed because few of its members, and among them no great power, really believed in or supported it, and which was from the beginning hopelessly handicapped by the refusal of America to join it. That was John's view — as it is mine.

If the League was defective and ineffective, the Secretariat, in some sort its reflection, was equally so. John never concealed his opinion that the Secretariat could not but be gravely hampered in its work by the jealousy and suspicion with which the Foreign Offices of the various Members of the League were certain to regard it. If the Secretariat were to perform more than minor functions of a routine character, it was bound to tread upon the toes of some *diplomate de carrière* in Paris, London, Berlin, Rome or other capital, and the reaction would be immediate and powerful.

Once again John was right, to what exact degree he learnt only after many years when, on joining the section of the Secretariat dealing with traffic in opium and other dangerous drugs, he was at last given a certain amount of responsibility. There he could, and did, measure the lengths to which Government departments of every nation are accustomed to go in order to conceal an awkward fact, to muddle or postpone the reply to a too pertinent question and, when all else fails, to cloud the issue by a discharge of ink, in the manner of a certain marine creature which, mentioned in their connection, should bear the name of scuttle-fish.

The Secretariat of the League of Nations, of which John was a member for twenty years, was a curious collection of men and women divided roughly into masters and helots. The first class was made up of representatives of almost every nationality except British and French, of whom there were very few, while the second, save for a sprinkling of local Swiss, was composed of no one else. There were two reasons, the first mechanical, the second political, to account for a state of affairs which prevented all but one or two of the many able and sincere Englishmen and Frenchmen — John not the least among them — from reaching positions worthy of their ideals and abilities. The official languages were French and English, and only those whose mother tongue was one or the other could be employed in the work of translating documents, interpreting speeches and recording proceedings. This huge drudgery fell inevitably upon the helots, the French and English, who had to be numerous, for the amount of work was very great, and subordinate, because they were nationals of two great powers and it must never be said, or thought, that Britain and France were seeking to dominate the League through their citizens serving on the Secretariat. True, on joining, every official was supposed to relinquish all national ties, and later on the higher grades were required to take an oath by which they undertook to serve the League and not their own country ; but it was felt that, human nature being what it is, it was better to run no risks and to secure, by as diverse a representation of nationalities as possible, that impartial spirit, lacking which a servant of the League was no better than an agent or even a spy. That, to write the bald truth, was what more than one of them was, and that is one of the main reasons why the Secretariat failed so lamentably and so tragically. A thin and tattered cloak of internationalism covered feelings of patriotism of the most rampant and extravagant kind, and for that *esprit de corps* without which no corporate undertaking can flourish and grow strong, was substituted an *esprit de couloir* as blatant as any which exists in less pretentious institutions. Far too many Members of Section, as the higher grade of official was called, had eyes on their own countries to have any real loyalty towards the international body which paid them their salaries.

The nationals of the Fascist states were the worst offenders. Very few of them were more than agents of their governments seconded for a term of years to the Secretariat from Government service to which they would ultimately return, ostensibly to cope with all kinds of international problems affecting the whole or a great part of the world, but in reality for the purpose of keeping a sharp eye upon, and furthering the interests of, their native land whenever they could. Nor were many of the nationals of lesser powers ignorant of the same practice. It is hard to blame such persons too severely. They had their future to think about, for their term of office with the League was limited, and they well knew what would be their fate on their return to their own homes if they had not put their country first when wallowing amid the fleshpots of Geneva. There were, of course, many honourable exceptions, but the great majority of these came from Scandinavia and northern Europe, where a wider spirit has long prevailed.

I do not think John ever became used to the Secretariat,

where in official hours there was a tendency to treat him as a man apart. He said very little, but when asked for his opinion gave it fully and fearlessly. Perhaps it was for that reason that it was not asked for very often. " *Ce sacré Palmer, on ne sait jamais ce qu'il pense et, quand enfin il parle, il dit des choses impossibles,*" once exclaimed the Italian Under-Secretary, whose name and titles — he called himself the Marquis Paolucci di Calboli Barone — were as impressive as his appearance and abilities were ludicrous.

Before joining the opium section, John served a long term as a Minute-writer with others and myself as his assistants. It was our job to keep the Minutes of the numerous Committees by which the work of the League was frustrated. They were of all kinds, and the length of their deliberations varied inversely with their importance. Thus, during the early years, the Council sat in Olympian calm, seldom for more than two hours at a stretch. Its Members often devoted them to sleep — it was once suggested by the Spanish delegate, Señor Quinones de León, that the Council's dignity when in session would be improved if its Members had an open eye painted on each eyelid — lulled into this condition by the wordy bickerings of the representatives of quarrelsome and quarrelling countries allergic alike to counsel or command.

Other Committees were less somnolent and sat for days chattering about opium and dangerous drugs, or obscene publications, or double taxation, or almost any other ill that flesh is heir to, and we would sit at a little table amid them and take notes of their unending and rarely conclusive deliberations. There could be nothing more calculated to damp the ardour of an idealist such as John, than that duty of recording the commonplace or partisan remarks made by the average member of a League of Nations Committee. There were exceptions, of course, and occasions

when a great man like Fridtjof Nansen, or Robert Cecil, or
Aristide Briand, spoke his mind, but they were as rare as
snow in May and not much more profitable. The pity of
it for John as for others, whose hatred of war was as intense
as is the passion of the Germans for it, was the flicker of
hope that ever and anon arose, a thin flame, from embers
never properly kindled. Thus, when the Assembly of 1924,
led by Herriot and MacDonald, the heads of two weak
but very sincere Governments of the Left, drafted the
Geneva protocol, John's spirits rose. It was a genuine
attempt to " put teeth " into the Covenant by defining in
detail, which went far beyond the general wording of
Article XVI, the exact obligations of States Members in
the event of a breach of the Covenant, and which auto-
matically pilloried the aggressor in a noteworthy phrase of
Benes as " that party to a dispute which refuses arbitration ".

The night the protocol was adopted by the Assembly
without, I believe, a dissentient vote, John and the rest of
us worked with hearts grown suddenly light to ensure that
a full record of what he believed at the time was a moment-
ous sitting should appear next morning in the *Assembly
Journal*, of which he was the editor. A day or two later
the captains and the kings departed, and next year their
place was taken by a cold, monocled individual, listened to
in icy silence by the representatives of fifty nations, as he
damned with faint praise the efforts of their predecessors,
and on behalf of His Majesty's Government consigned the
protocol to the wastepaper basket. John always regarded
the attitude adopted that day by Austen Chamberlain as an
act of the blackest treachery towards mankind. In the light
of what his brother [1] accomplished at Munich in 1938, and
of the carnage of 1939 to 1945, not to mention that of the

[1] " To know him ", John once averred, " must be a Secondary
Education."

Japanese war, who is to say with justice that John's verdict was wrong ?

Again, in 1927, when under the impulse of that far-seeing economist, Sir Arthur Salter, a conference of the world's leading economists met by the shores of Lake Leman, John was for the moment full of hope. But those experts, though acknowledged to be among the greatest in the world in their special field, represented no government and had no official authority. Perhaps that was why their report was so striking and certainly, as John remarked, why no government paid any attention to it. All their prophecies came true in less than two years, when the great slump of 1929 fell upon the world, and it only needed the tragic farce of the World Monetary and Economic Conference of 1933, which John also attended, to point the inevitable and dreary moral.

The last time I saw him hopeful was in the early days of the Disarmament Conference of 1932. Arthur Henderson was its president and John was appointed his official secretary. A bond of respect and affection was soon forged between the two men, alike in their transcendent and transparent honesty and in their horror of war. By then intrigues in front, upon, and behind the scenes were of little significance to John. He was used to them, but never did his habit of silence stand him in better stead. The uneasy, uncertain British, the crude Germans, the subtle, timorous French, the posturing Italians, the earnest, suspicious Americans, the chattering representatives of the lesser powers, none could throw dust in John's shrewd eyes. He reported faithfully and accurately all he heard, all he saw, to " Uncle Arthur ". Rarely has the president of a conference been better informed, never better served. For a few brief days in the spring of 1932, when the British and French Prime Ministers, the Italian Foreign Minister and the German Chancellor were all in Geneva at the same time,

John believed that something at last might be accomplished. The opportunity, if it ever really existed, faded almost before it appeared, and when, a few months later, Hitler assumed power in Berlin, it was obvious to persons far less perspicacious than John, that all was lost.

I have dwelt at some length on the official side of John's life because, writer though he was by inclination, he had, by the necessities of his profession, to spend many hours of every day at an official, not a writer's desk. Any description of those hours cannot but be depressing, for, through no fault of his own, he was associated for twenty years with an enterprise which might have been great but which failed and brought with its failure the disaster of a second world war. But John himself was not by temperament a prophet of woe and the effect of his personality on his friends was the opposite of depressing. Despite his official surroundings, he was from first to last an optimist, for his love of mankind and his belief in the essential nobility of man's nature were too strong to be shaken. That

> The pale, pathetic peoples still plod on,
> Through hoodwinkings to light

was a saying of Thomas Hardy which he often quoted and in which he firmly believed, and the quiet cynicism, which he could display when he so wished with devastating effect, sprang from no more than a prolonged and enforced acquaintance with the less attractive qualities of his fellow-men. Too gentle to display indignation at the constant exhibition of them in the whispering corridors or wide Committee rooms of the Secretariat building, he chose instead silence in the office and, outside it, devoted every moment that he could to literature and music, two arts which were twin realities in a world of uneasy dreaming.

From the very beginning of our friendship John was insistent that, however remarkable or repellent the glories and grandeurs, the foibles and follies of the politicians, diplomats, journalists, philanthrophists *et hoc genus omne* who swarmed in Geneva might be, the essentials of life — music and the theatre, poetry and art — were still to be had even in the city of Calvin, if one looked for them. It was he who took me to see the Pitoëffs in the early days of their career when, up to the eyes in debt, they were producing Shakespeare, Wilde, Ibsen and Lenormand. In those days, for the equivalent of half a crown, you could see Ludmilla Pitoëff, one of the greatest actresses of the world, play Hedda Gabler to a theatre two-thirds empty, for it was not until ten years later, when they had made a name for themselves in Paris, that the Genevese flocked to see them and were required, I am glad to say, to pay five times as much.

John's love of the theatre was insatiable, and with Paris distant only a day or a night's journey, he was enabled to keep in reasonably close touch with it at a time when men like Jouvet, Gaston Baty and Dullin were worthily maintaining the traditions of the French stage. In 1927 he published a volume of *Studies in the Contemporary Theatre*, and the writing of these together with a number of articles on the French stage revived his dormant interest in its most famous exponent, Molière, whose biography he presently began to write. It appeared in 1930 and showed John at his best as an interpreter of the mind of one who was not only a playwright but also a philosopher and a poet. John loved Molière and, what is more, understood him. Across the years that separated them John flung a bridge which he was wont to cross whenever he felt in need of contact with a kindred spirit, and his admiration of the brilliant playwright and actor, whose wit and charm concealed a

heart full of charity even for those whose foibles and hypo-
crisies he so mercilessly exposed in his plays, was exceeded
only by an even greater admiration and understanding of
Shakespeare. John was describing his own emotions when,
in a novel of the seventeenth century which he and I wrote
together, he depicted the effect on James de la Cloche, the
hero, of a first meeting with Jean-Baptiste Poquelin, com-
monly known as the Sieur de Molière :

There was something about this man that touched him to
the heart. The face, which a moment before had assumed the
comic mask, was now at rest, the dark eyes full of a wistful
knowledge, the sensitive mouth faintly smiling upon some secret
thought, as though he had stepped suddenly from the world
into a sad seclusion.

It might also be a self-portrait, for such was the
impression John so often made on those about him. Not
that he was of a melancholy habit ; it was only that he was
observant and preferred, whenever he could assume it, the
part of onlooker. Tolerant and warm-hearted, he knew the
value alike of silence and of speech, using both to comfort,
never to inflict a hurt. In this he differed somewhat from
Molière, whom he depicts in his biography as a man possessed of a passionate sincerity which led him to reject the
second-rate wherever and whenever he met with it. So
did John, but with this difference. Having encountered
it, his protest was made in so kindly a fashion as never to
cause a wound.

The biography of Molière proclaimed John Palmer to
be as great an authority on French as he was on English
playwrights of the seventeenth century. It was followed by
a life of Ben Jonson, whom he described as " the greatest
of English worthies ", the indomitable leader of a great,
but lost, cause — one which John had deeply at heart, the
cause of intellectual light. In his eyes, Jonson

is the principal English figure in the European tragedy which ended in the defeat of the scholars, when the mediaeval mind, emerging into the sunlight, was thrust back into the shadows. He belonged to a generation which had listened to Erasmus. He survived into the generation of Praise-God-Barebones. Of that generation we are still essentially the heirs. England has not yet recovered her inheritance. Every now and then comes a period of the fidgets, but the superficial freedoms, on which we pride ourselves today, are little more than the perambulations of a hungry beast in a cage. We are still strangers in Bartholomew Fair.

Are these words, written in 1934, less true today ? I do not think so. They are wise words, to which the teachers of youth in this country would do well to pay heed. Learning does not spring from Education Acts like Athene fully armed from the head of Zeus. That a little of it is a dangerous thing has become a trite saying only because the years have abundantly proved the wisdom of Pope's aphorism. It was ever present in John's mind. He hated slipshod work, the product of a quick glance at the appropriate article in the *Encyclopædia Britannica*. Himself a scholar of Balliol, he enjoyed the company of men who had a scholarly approach to life, and was therefore happy when attending the meetings of the Committee on Intellectual Co-operation. Though its members were quite impractical and spent many hours in talk which was brilliant just because, largely for political reasons, it led, and could lead, nowhere, they were the finest intelligences of the age. I remember his fascinated delight at the conversation of Bergson at a luncheon party which lasted three hours and a half and made him very late for the afternoon meeting. At various times, too, he met Madame Curie, Paul Valéry, Gilbert Murray, and once, Olympian and aloof, Einstein. These intellectual giants were scarcely more than acquaintances, but John rejoiced when he was in their company, for they were the men and women who had come " by striving into Troy town ", who, in their own persons, were the latest flowering of the tree of know-ledge and who in the last resort were at once the excuse and the justification of the human race. Their presence in Geneva, whence had streamed out that dark cloud upon which rode Calvin, like the djinn from the bottle, over-whelming the Renaissance and robbing us of an inheritance we " have not yet recovered ", was for him as for others an ironic twist of Fortune's wheel.

The materialism rife in Geneva among its moneyed classes had no appeal for John, but among those for whom the pursuit of money was not the pursuit of happiness he had many friends : Ansermet, the conductor of the Orchestre Romande ; René Louis Piachaud, the poet, whose trans-lation of *Coriolanus* caused a riot in Paris when it was produced by the Français ; the music teachers of that gifted player of the violin, his daughter ; Fournier, the struggling director of the Comédie, Geneva's local theatre, and others.

He responded to the beauty of Geneva as a town but the countryside around it was his delight. He loved to walk or ride and, on autumn and winter mornings, to run over it, for he was an assiduous follower of Tony Buxton's beagles, unique of their kind on the Continent, and as enthusiastic and incompetent a whip as I was. Waiting in the very early dawn of an October day at the corner of a vineyard from which the grapes had just been plucked, or, in January, on the edge of an oak copse with the breath of winter sharp upon it, and behind, fifty miles away, Mont Blanc, " alone and very valorous in his isolation ", we would argue about the form and substance of a new chapter of *The Six Proud Walkers* or *Death Walks in Eastrepps* or whatever thriller was on the stocks at the moment. Then would come a sudden whimper and a change of note in Tony's cries of encouragement, and then the voices of his hounds, full-throated, and then the urgent call of his horn across the shadowy meadows and we would throw back our heads and run.

Even more memorable were the runs on skis, followed by an evening of pleasant carousal as members of the *Société Gastronomique et des Sports d'Hiver* which John and I founded. It was a merry club in which the splendours of ski-ing, the drinking of wine — the entrance fee was six bottles of burgundy of a vintage year — and the maintenance of good conversation were suitably blended.

As a ski-er John was indefatigable. He loved the mountains of High Savoy and the good fellowship which is bred by traversing their noble slopes on skis. To write of winter sports in connection with John must inevitably recall our first holiday which we spent at Engelberg in January 1921. Neither of us at that date knew anything about ski-ing or bobbing, and not very much about skating. In those days Engelberg possessed a famous bob-run cut in the ice and snow of the Gerschner Alp and shaped not unlike the brand of lightning Jove clutches in a Tiepolo ceiling. I had been down it twice on a kind of highly mobile scavenger's daughter, called, not altogether inappropriately, a skeleton. John had preferred the more comfortable and less lethal luge. Having reached the bottom separately and safely, we felt we knew all about manning a boblet together, and that night, flown with the contagious insolence of a very poor type we had met at the hotel bar and the wine we had drunk there, we entered for the boblet race of the morrow.

The morning found us resolute but inwardly fearful — at least I was, for the vehicle we had rashly undertaken to ride was not reassuring. It was a low iron sled, supported on steel runners of which the front pair could be turned to right or left by means of hawsers ending in handles. Hinged to the back of the boblet was a set of grinning steel teeth which, in theory at least, bit the ice on the jerking of a pair of levers. Who should handle which? We tossed; John won and decided that control of the braking mechanism rather than the steering was his *forte*. As it turned out, the choice was unfortunate, for in leaping on to the back of the boblet which, by the rules, he had to push in order to start on its way, John slipped, landed face downwards upon it and lost his spectacles. For him that breakneck journey was, as he said afterwards, " a moving mist through which I sometimes saw huge fingers. I suppose they were fir trees ". My own vision was clearer. I could see the sun glinting on the high-banked curves, to shoot over which meant a heavy fall, a broken limb, perhaps worse, the ringing ice, blue in the shadow of the trees, the faces of the spectators, all teeth and eyes. But what I saw most clearly was the marks of the brakes which other competitors had jammed on before negotiating each successive curve. I shouted for them to be applied in our case. I could not hear John's reply because of the balaclava helmet over my ears, but there was no slackening of speed, not the whole way down, though I yelled for the brakes at every curve; not even a response to my last despairing cry as we shot out of the run through the station of the funicular railway, scattering porters and fellow tourists to right and left, to finish smartly in a frozen stream — not frozen enough — into which we plunged and stopped at last. " What happened to the brakes ? " I enquired in great wrath after I had got my head free of the balaclava. "Wouldn't work, old boy. I tugged in vain," answered John. This was serious. To have allowed two novices to race on a defective machine. . . . I raised and lowered the brake levers. The teeth at the end of them bit the foot of a kindly rescuer; he lifted up his voice and swore. They seemed to be in perfect order. " Oh," said John thoughtfully, " I never saw those. I was tugging at this," and he indicated the leather thong which the brakesman clutches when swinging round a curve. We won third prize, beat the braggart at the bar and highly gratified the designer of the bob-run, who maintained that we had proved that an uncontrolled boblet would descend it without mishap, so perfectly was it banked and graded. After that day we took to ski-ing.

His books on Molière and Ben Jonson, and his many articles on the theatre and on French literature published in *The Times Literary Supplement*, though they enhanced his reputation among men of letters, did not bring John any wide recognition. It was his studies of certain *Political Characters of Shakespeare*, a book which appeared six months after his death, which established his reputation as a Shakespearian scholar and critic of the highest order. Into this book John put all the accumulated wisdom acquired during years devoted to the close and patient examination of politicians in action against an international background and all the understanding with which a lifelong study of Shakespeare had endowed him. The result is a most remarkable book in which the reader may study the habits, thoughts, actions and reactions of every kind of politician from Brutus, the earnest, honest, ineffective Liberal, to Richard III, the bold, calculating, brutal Dictator. They are all there, those types made familiar to us by film, newspaper and radio, dressed in curious clothes, perhaps, and speaking matchless verse or prose, but depicted to the life by a supreme genius and explained by an exceptionally observant and gifted writer.

It is small wonder that the *Political Characters of Shakespeare* has been so widely acclaimed. It is more than admirably informed criticism ; it is a political guide, written and published at a moment when the need for such a book has never been greater. John intended it to be the first of a trilogy on Shakespeare. The other two volumes were to deal in turn with his Comic and his Tragic characters. For the second only a few notes exist, but five of the Comic studies were left ready for publication. John did not live to enjoy that sweetest of all triumphs, the praise and recognition of his equals in the world of letters in which he had walked for thirty years.

He wrote the book in the rare intervals of leisure which his work for the British Broadcasting Corporation left him. He was on its staff for the last five years of his life, having left Geneva for London a few months before the outbreak of war in 1939. Those years when he had established himself in Hampstead, become a member of the Garrick Club, where he had many friends, and taken up the threads of a life he had, perforce, abandoned so many years before, were among the happiest of his life, despite the burden of the war which he had so long foreseen. After a month or two with the Ministry of Information, he joined the European News Service where his great knowledge of affairs and the acquired experience of his long sojourn in Geneva proved invaluable. The success of Colonel Britton and the V sign owed very much to his efforts and his imagination. The hours of work were long and the daily toil arduous, but he knew that he was doing good service and, though the battle raged and the " pale, pathetic peoples " were paying a grim price for the hoodwinkings of twenty years, he was oddly content and at peace.

Nor was this frame of mind disturbed by the first onset of the malady which was to kill him and which was checked but not cured by an operation in 1942. It was while lying in hospital recovering that he solved the meaning of music as applied to himself. He talked much to me of this, a mystical experience which befell him in the midst of great physical pain and which gave him profound joy and an inner peace that was with him to the end of his life two years later. I think he reached, through pondering on Beethoven's symphonies, of which, trained musician as he was, he had a profound understanding, the same state of mind reached by others through the medium of prayer and contemplation. Beethoven led him into a world which is as indefinable as it is real, a world that he himself knew well, and which Ruysbroek knew, and St. John of the Cross, and El Greco, and Vaughan, and all the other mystical writers, musicians, painters and poets, a world into whose confines John passed with the hand of death almost upon him. At that time we were completing *The Grand Design*, and its hero, James de la Cloche, had just encountered a curious and fascinating person, Hugh Cressy, the Oxford scholar, turned Catholic, who had much to do with the attempts made in the middle of the seventeenth century to bring England back to Rome. Into Cressy's mouth John put words which *mutatis mutandis* described his own most happy state of mind :

Let your heart be constant, for within it is the divine fortress which defends and protects you, a strong castle whose garrison is Divine Aid and Sovereign Succour. To this fortress Christ will return to quiet you. . . . Within your heart, by the aid of His heavenly grace, you may find silence in tumult, solitude in company, light in darkness, vigour in despondency, courage in fear, resistance in temptation, peace in war, and quiet in times of unrest.

In May 1944 a second operation was found necessary, and after ten weeks of great pain unflinchingly endured, a sudden haemorrhage occurred at midnight on the 5th August and John Leslie Palmer died.

For his wife who survived him only some eighteen months and for his children he left an abiding memory of love and sweetness; for me the memory of a friendship, faultless and flawless, which illumined twenty-four years of life. Its radiance is upon me still, and will fade only with consciousness itself. His spirit was gentle, his judgement serene, his love prodigal.

I wear him in my heart's core.

The First Encounter

§ 1

NO, Gaston, that is not the sabre with which I cut off the head of the Grand Duke Constantine at the battle of Austerlitz. I have never cut off anyone's head, little savage. That's what the Emperor called Mustapha, his Mameluke, for it was he who made the threat about the Grand Duke, not your old grandfather. What's that? No, of course I wasn't an old man then, Suzanne, and had you been sitting on my knee on Christmas Day 1805 instead of 1855, I should hardly have known that you were there. Now then, little hussy, keep still. You mustn't wriggle in the saddle if you want to ride in the way the granddaughter of a Light Cavalryman should. Steady. Steady. That's better.

Now where was I? Oh, my sabre. Yes, Gaston, it did belong to my father, who had it from his, and it is of the finest Solingen steel, for it was made long ago in the seventeenth century, when they knew how to forge blades. Yes, I did have it with me at Austerlitz, I admit it. It is usual for a soldier to have his weapon in his hand when he is engaged in a battle. But I did not, I repeat, cut anyone's . . . What? Speak up, my darling. A soft voice, gentle and low, may be an excellent thing in woman, as the playwright Shakespeare says somewhere — he was a kind of English Racine and Molière combined and hardly worth reading — but I find a woman's voice nowadays is merely a mumble. Oh, what was the first time I used my father's sabre? Ah, that's what you'd like to know, is it? Well, to speak

1

the truth I am not very proud of the first time, though it's a long while ago now. But when one is a General of Division with seven wounds and eight medals, one can laugh at the follies of an eighteen-year-old trooper.

For that's how I began, my dears. Oh yes, your old grandfather started his career in the ranks like all the Emperor's famous soldiers and most of his Marshals. Only he wasn't the Emperor then — not for many years afterwards — eight to be correct. For I'm speaking of the spring of 1796. I was not quite turned eighteen then and had been with the army only a month or two longer than General Bonaparte, as he was then called, who was commanding it. What army? Now, Gaston, if you continue to interrupt, it will be your bedtime before I'm half-way through. So, quiet please, and at the end you may draw the sabre once, just as I drew it that spring afternoon on the sands near the smelly Italian port of Savona.

As I have told you, I was a mere trooper at the time, even though my father — your great-grandfather — was a General. But we all went through the ranks whatever our birth or station in life. Indeed there weren't any more births or stations by then, for the Revolution was already seven years old and had abolished all that. It was guts that counted in the army, not birth and brains, not station. Well, I believe I have my share of both, as my present rank and my long career have shewn; but in those days both were before me and I hadn't heard a shot fired in anger except the one discharged at a footpad by the coach guard in the forest of Fontainebleau when I was on my way south from Paris to join my regiment. It was the Hussars of Angers and they were in cantonments on the French-Genoese frontier. A tough lot were the Hussars of Angers even

2

for cavalrymen and feared neither God nor the devil, nor General Scherer who had commanded the army before Bonaparte took over, and they were only a trifle put-out by our brigadier Macard whose conduct on the field of battle was perhaps a thought bizarre. On seeing the enemy this singular man, whose size was as colossal as his bravery, was wont to shout, " I shall fight as a beast," and to tear off all his clothes down to the waist, thus presenting a truly formidable spectacle. For he was covered with hair, my children, like a bear, a huge, brown bear, and in this costume, supplied by nature and embellished by art — for he continued to wear his General's plumed hat — he would charge the enemy with inconceivable ferocity. They seldom awaited his coming. So you see, with that sort of man to lead the hussars of the army, we were not exactly lambs. We were indeed wolves and we did not bother about sheep's clothing.

One thing we all had in common besides bravery and a total lack of pay, and that was moustaches. There were black ones and red ones and brown ones and grey ones and a few white — but we all had them — had to have them indeed. That was the order. They had to be long and curled upwards so that the points ended only just below the eyes. Now, as I have said, my children, I was not yet eighteen and therefore still a youth — a pretty little tart my *mentor* called me, but don't repeat that expression to your dear mother — and nature had not yet allowed me to grow moustaches on the same scale as the rest. What was a *mentor* ? Yes, I'm coming to that. He was an old soldier and his job was to take two or three of the young ones in hand and teach 'em the ropes. A remarkable man was my *mentor* — you might say formidable and not be guilty of

3

exaggeration. His name was Pasquier and I shall never forget him. He was killed at Friedland when I had left the Hussars of Angers for Augereau's staff. But that spring morning when we first met at the Crowing Cock, a miserable little drink-shop outside Savona which sold a kind of vinegar that the landlord had the impertinence to call wine, he was very much alive. I saw before me a giant, well turned out it is true, in a clean, if worn, uniform — green with yellow facings, the Regiment's colours — but with his shako at a rakish angle over one eye and the end of his sabre's sheath trailing in the dust. Of his face the most notable features were a huge scar which bisected it transversely from forehead to chin, and a pair of the largest moustaches I have ever seen. They were half a foot long, stiffened with wax, and lost themselves in his ears. From his forehead depended two locks of hair which, tumbling from his shako, fell one each side of his face and ended on his chest. With all this he had an air — well, a swaggering, boisterous demeanour it was, yet illumined by some deeper quality which I could perceive but not describe.

" Holy Blue, where are your moustaches, recruit ? " were his first words, and before I could explain — and, my children, explanations were not really necessary — he had whipped me off to the horse lines, procured a pot of black wax and affixed to my young face two moustaches almost as big as his own. " Stick to these, recruit," he growled, " or . . ." But it seemed only too probable that they would stick to me.

" Yes," I answered meekly, " and when I wash ? "

" The Hussars of Angers don't wash," he answered. " We leave that to the filthy English whom you'll meet one day when we have our revenge for Toulon." He spoke with bitterness, you understand, because it was

4

at the siege of that port that he had been wounded by a shot from a British man-of-war.

Those moustaches were a trial at all times but especially in the hot weather. We had no brims to our shakos and the kisses of the Mediterranean sun were fierce — so fierce that on parade the wax was apt to melt and pull the skin of my face in a highly irritating manner and I could do nothing. I couldn't move a muscle, you understand. Not on parade ; not as an hussar.

About all that Pasquier taught me I will not go into details. It must suffice that I learnt to do a great deal more for a horse than merely to saddle and bridle him, and a great deal more for arms and a uniform than merely to wear them. I was an apt pupil, though I say it who shouldn't, and was soon on terms with my " old soldier ", even going so far as to acquire, if not a taste, at least a tolerance for the red, sour wine of the country of which Pasquier was accustomed to consume vast quantities — at my expense. For this there was plenty of opportunity. The French army, what there was of it, was echeloned from Savona down the coast to Loano and thence to Nice, while inland detachments stretched up the mountains as far as the Col de Tende. There were some forty-two thousand of us, and I doubt if there was a sound pair of boots in the whole army, while the money General Bonaparte raised from a local banker in Nice was the first pay most of the men had had for more than a year.

But if we were ragged, we were tough, and not all the money in the world could stop an hussar — or, for that matter, an infantryman — from drinking the wine of the country. Pasquier, I and others of the *Clique* were wont to do so in the Crowing Cock. The *Clique*, I should explain, was what you might call the inner circle of the Hussars of Angers. It was made up of all the ragamuffins of the Regiment and also of the bravest men. We had a pact to uphold each other on all occasions, but especially in the face of the enemy. We called ourselves the Wags and were forever playing jokes. What's that, Gaston? Tossing in horse blankets? That's a very mild sort of joke compared with those in which we used to indulge.

The Wags were to be distinguished by a mark cut with a knife on the top button of the right-hand row of those which adorned our tunics. We were a wild lot, and the Knights of the Scarred Button, as our poet, young Vigier, called us until he was cut in two by a cannon-ball in front of Ulm, were foremost alike in battle and in the farmyard. We were the finest scroungers of the whole army. I don't mind telling you I was mad to join the *Clique*. I thought of nothing else, but it was not easy. I had as yet, as I have said, heard no shot fired in anger. I had, you understand, to prove myself, and though I got hold of a couple of geese and a turkey in a somewhat unusual manner which went some way towards establishing my reputation, I had yet to prove my worth when face to face with the enemy. And as the days drew out into weeks and we made no move against the Austrians, I became more and more desperate. There was a lot of talk in March about our new young General; Napoleon Bonaparte, his name was, and he had taken over from that whining old ruffian, Scherer, who was always more ready with complaints than with a plan of battle. But he was a dark horse, Bonaparte. No one knew anything about him. We hadn't even seen him, and his name was, of course, against him, an outlandish Italian name, better suited, so young Vigier said, to some warrior of Italian romance, some companion of Orlando Furioso, rather than to a commander of a French army in the field.

Be that as it may, we were all chafing at our existence, endless drill alternating with field exercises which the Colonel — Bassompierre his name was — carried out whenever the horses were fit enough, for there was a deplorable lack of forage and we could not work them too hard. And in the lengthening afternoons there was much drinking in the wine-shops, especially at the Crowing Cock. It was there, towards the end of the month, that my first adventure really began. As I have said, I was desperately keen to join the *Clique* and I used to go about as much as I could in their company, for, of course, old Pasquier was one of them, but I had not yet dared to cut the coveted scar on the top right-hand button of my tunic.

Well, one day — it was fairly early in the afternoon, for, for some reason, parades had been cancelled — I entered the Crowing Cock at the heels of Pasquier. It was fuller than usual, with many different types belonging to the army. There were green-clad Voltigeurs, blue-coated infantrymen, and blue-and-white gunners, all of them ragged, all of them thirsty. It was one of these last who began it all, a great big fellow he was. After all these years I have forgotten his name, but he was seated in his shirt-sleeves, the great muscles of his thighs straining every seam of his stained white riding breeches. He belonged to the Horse Gunners, or Flying Artillery as they were called, and he was leaning perilously back on a tilted stool when Pasquier and I entered the wine-shop. We were hussars, as I have said, and no hussar moves a yard without his sabre. In those days there was no hook to our sword-belts, so that it was not possible to hitch the sabre up. When you were out of

7

the saddle you had either to carry it in your hand or let it trail along the ground, when the end of the sheath clattered and rang against the cobbles and paving stones of the way and made an infernal din which was music in the ears of a light cavalryman.

As I pushed past the gunner my sabre was trailing at the proper angle. Bump, bump, it went over the dirty, wine-stained boards till it struck one of the legs of his stool. Now I won't say it was design and I won't say it was accident, but at that moment I put my hand on the hilt and my hand was heavy. This gesture set in motion the sabre and the sheath embracing it. The end struck the stool legs sharply. I have already said that the gunner was precariously balanced. That little blow was, so to speak, the last straw on the camel's back. The stool jerked suddenly forward, the backside of the big gunner slid heavily off it and crashed to the floor, while the contents of the wine-glass he had in his hand at the time were distributed over his stomach. Yes, Suzanne, he was indeed a ridiculous sight, and you may well laugh. But he, he did not laugh. For a moment he sat there gazing stupidly round, then his eye lit on Pasquier standing over him, a grim smile on his face.

" You," roared the artilleryman, and then stopped short, as well he might, for Pasquier presented a formidable appearance. Those huge moustaches of his bristled like the horns of an ox. He was as large as, if not larger than, the gunner and the scar across his face added more to its ferocity than to its beauty. The eyes of the gunner shifted from Pasquier to myself, standing half a pace behind him. The gunner pursed his lips.

" You," he said, and his finger pointed at me. " Hussar, you let your sabre drag on the ground far too much." As he spoke he got clumsily to his feet.

8

I did not answer him. Pasquier had not deigned to notice him and I was bent on imitating Pasquier in every particular. I was moving past, leaving my sabre where it was, still trailing that is, intent on joining some comrades at a near-by table, when Pasquier whispered in my ear out of the corner of his mouth : " Tell him to come and pick it up for you."

" Come and pick it up, then, gunner," I heard myself say.

" That's an easy job, baby," roared the gunner, and he stretched out a huge hand.

I drew myself up, and as it approached the hilt of my sabre I struck it sharply aside. My children, that blow was enough. In an instant the room was in an uproar. Pasquier had the gunner by the throat and half a dozen of the *Clique* were locked with an equal number of gunners. The table went over with a crash, a jug splintered and the red wine spread, a dark pool, on the dirty floor.

§ 2

It was a sergeant who called himself Dubois who stopped the *mêlée*. His real name I never knew, but he was undoubtedly, like myself, a scion of the old régime, in other words a member of the smaller nobility who up till 1789 had enjoyed the privileges which rank and the possession of land conferred. Like me he had decided to serve France rather than his own faction, and he had remained in the country through all the troubled years which followed that famous May meeting of the Estates in the tennis-court at Versailles. But he had thought it prudent to change his name for reasons which concerned only himself. His voice, in which a note of firm, unquestioning authority was to be heard, rang out in that crowded wine-shop.

"Gentlemen, we must settle this matter in due and proper form. Stop savaging each other, I pray you. You, trooper, what's your name?"

He was speaking to me, and as I disengaged myself with some difficulty from the embraces of a gunner friend of the gunner whom I must admit I had provoked, I found myself within a foot of him.

"Armand de Blanchegarde," I replied, for unlike the sergeant I had kept my own name. Well, after all, your great-grandfather was a General serving under the Republic — but that's neither here nor there.

"And yours?" said Sergeant Dubois, looking at the great gunner still in the grip of my *mentor*.

The colossus growled out a name which, as I say, I have forgotten.

"We must have no more brawling here," continued Dubois. "You will, I trust, settle this affair like gentlemen."

His tone, crisp and emphatic, induced a momentary silence. It would be wrong to say that you could have heard a pin drop, but the shouts and oaths died away and men stared at each other with flushed faces and bared teeth.

"Certainly," I said, swallowing once. "I am perfectly ready to give this gentleman any satisfaction he may desire."

"And you?"

The colossus made a noise between a growl and a belch which Sergeant Dubois evidently took to be an answer in the affirmative, for he continued: "I suggest the meeting should not be postponed for . . . er . . . obvious reasons, and we should therefore adjourn at once to the seashore. 'Tis but a moment's walk from here and will, I fancy, be very convenient."

The words were hardly out of his mouth when the silence he had induced was broken by a general murmur of assent, and in a body we moved in the direction which he had indicated.

I said, my children, that I swallowed once in my throat, but I swallowed again when I walked out of the wine-shop with Pasquier at my side. Not that I was afraid of the giant gunner. You must believe me when I say that I was not. After all, I was nearly eighteen and I had been learning the use of the small-sword since the age of twelve, while Pasquier himself had spent the previous month or so teaching me how to wield a sabre. That I could hold my own against a great hulking gunner more accustomed to hitching and unhitching the trace of the miniature cart-horse which dragged his bronze monster to the battlefield, I made no doubt. But — this was the trouble — duelling was forbidden. The army order about it had been promulgated as far back as a year before and it had been repeated more than once. Up to a month or two previously, it had remained more or less a dead letter and the number of duels fought had been very considerable. The French, as you may have observed, my children, are a pugnacious people, quick to back their opinions with arms on any and every suitable occasion, and on not a few that are perhaps not quite so suitable. But since the arrival of General Bonaparte things in the army in Italy had altered. His first act had been to disband an infantry battalion for mutinous conduct, and that gesture set the tone, as you might say, of the whole force. It led natur-ally to a rigid prohibition of duelling. Looking back on it now after all these years, I can see that Bonaparte was right. France could not afford to lose the service of a single man of courage, and it was only such as these who engaged in duels. Therefore they were prohibited under severe penalties. Yet here was I, committed by the quiet, inexorable Sergeant Dubois, with his rigid notions derived from the *ancien régime*, to an immediate encounter with sabres. Yet could I in honour draw back ? Could I plead army orders as an excuse for refusing to meet the gigantic gunner ? Well, I suppose I could, but I confess to you, my children, that such a thought crossed my mind only to be instantly rejected. The de Blanchegardes have ever been quick to defend their honour in any and every circumstance, and who was I to use an order, however reasonable, as a shield between me and what was, I thought, a family duty ? Thus, my dear Gaston, are we deceived, and remember always that those who put family above country are unworthy of the name of patriot. It was that tendency which was so fatal to the *émigrés* and which came so near to ruin France.

On that March afternoon, however, this was a lesson I had not yet learnt, and so I strode down to the seashore just west of that dirty little port of Savona, with my chin thrust out, my head high, and my ears open only to the hoarse advice of Pasquier telling me to aim at the great brute's chest and to watch, not his eyes, but his sword hand.

In due course we arrived at the seashore. Yes, Suzanne, it was a pleasant place, a long stretch of sand with the sea rippling very gently at its margin. Yes, you could certainly paddle and sail boats in it, but we were not there for that purpose. The sun was declining a trifle towards the west, for I suppose it must have been between four and five o'clock in the afternoon, and he, therefore, who fought with it at his back, or rather over

12

his right shoulder, had perhaps a trifling advantage. Who should be given this was decided by the spin of a coin. The gunner was the winner and accordingly he took his station opposite to me and began to brandish a sabre which seemed to my excited eyes to be about six feet long. While he was loosening his muscles I was taking off my coat and taking up my stand with my back to Savona and with the sea on my left hand. Pasquier had now fallen silent and was busying himself with making sure that the drawn sabre I held in my right hand should remain firmly in it, come what may. This end he secured by attaching it to my fist with a soiled cravat taken from his own neck. The operation completed, he advanced towards a small bombardier acting as second to my adversary, bowed clumsily and announced that his principal was ready to engage. Sergeant Dubois, who had assumed the rôle of Master of Ceremonies, if I may so describe it, called upon us to advance within sword's, or rather sabre's length. We did so, halting in front of each other and separated by a space just sufficient to enable us to salute and then fall to. How well I remember that moment! The sun in a sky flecked with light clouds, streamed in a slant upon the sand slightly, but by no means full in my eyes. The soft murmur of the sea made itself audible whenever the noise of talk from the onlookers ceased or died down. Their conversation was not of any great interest, being confined for the most part to bets in which the odds quoted were heavily against me.

" *En garde*," commanded Dubois crisply.

I raised my sabre and prepared to defend myself, for I had decided, my children, to let the gunner do the attacking. I would parry his cuts and thrusts, and when he tired seek to disarm him with a blow across the forearm or a thrust to the right shoulder.

I had, however, no opportunity to put this plan into practice. Our blades had not touched, though they were about to do so, when I saw a sudden expression of ludicrous dismay pass across the features of my antagonist. He was staring, not at me, but at something just beyond and behind me, and from the expression in his eyes he might have been confronted with the whole Austrian Army, horse, foot and guns, bearing down upon him at the charge. Anyway, he dropped his point, turned on his heel and bolted, yes, bolted, my children, as fast as his huge legs would carry him. And with him everyone else bolted too, all the gunners, all the hussars, all the members of the other regiments who formed the motley concourse gathered on the shore to witness our duel. Off they ran as though the fiend were at their heels, led by my defaulting gunner and Sergeant Dubois with Pasquier following closely in the rear. My children, I was bewildered. I stood there for a moment like a waxwork figure, my point still upraised, my body taut, and in the *en garde* position, and I was still in that position when a hand fell with the weight of lead on my right shoulder.

" Soldier, you are under arrest." The voice was hard and sharp. I dropped my point and wheeled round, just as another hand touched my right wrist and wrenched the sabre from my grasp. I found myself surrounded by a posse of Gendarmerie, a whole platoon it seemed to me of Military Police, tall, hard-faced men in blue uniforms, and, as I perceived them, my heart sank to my boots, for I knew who they were. The Gendarmerie are a fine corps, I would say no word against them. It was they whose first duty it was to preserve discipline in the armies of the Republic and the Empire, and this task they filled with great ability. Besides that, they were present at all the major battles and most of the minor ones, and gave a good account of themselves. Yes, a fine corps, but at that moment I could have wished them in hell or in the Antipodes. They had caught me fair and square and there was no escape. The others — I looked up. There they were, the whole crowd of them, running in a cloud of dust, or rather sand, as fast as they could.

"Who is this man ?" It was a new voice, a sharp, incisive voice with, it seemed to me, all the ice of Mont Blanc in it.

"What's your name ? Your name ?" The hoarse accents of a corporal of Gendarmerie sounded in my ear.

"Trooper de Blanchegarde," I found myself saying as I looked towards the origin of the icy voice.

I saw a small man, well below middle height, and not far past the middle twenties. A lock of black hair fell across an ivory forehead. His hollow cheeks were of the same hue but the clean-shaven hairs gave them a slightly bluish tinge. He was wearing the blue coat with white facings of a colonel of gunners, with a huge tricolour sash wound round his slim waist. But these details I no longer noticed as I saw his eyes. They were hard as marbles, yet fierce as diamonds. Their gaze pierced me through and through, and the mouth beneath the thin nose was set in a firm, unyielding line. I shook myself free of the corporal's restraining hand, drew myself up, and forgetting I had no shako on my head, saluted, for I realised I was in the presence of General Bonaparte.

There was a moment's utter silence, broken, I remember, only by the soft, insistent grumble of the sea. General Bonaparte took a pace forward. His hands went behind his back in a gesture soon to be famous throughout the world. His chin was thrust out.

" Duelling ? " he said in the same harsh tone.

I remained silent. At that moment I could not have spoken if the Archangel Gabriel had kicked my backside. That was the sort of effect, you understand, that the General had on one.

" Duelling ? " he repeated, and his voice had an Italian tang in it.

" Yes, *mon général*."

" Do you know the order ? "

" Yes, *mon général*."

" Take him to the Bishop's Palace. Let the court-martial assemble at dawn."

" Yes, *mon*——" I found myself saying, like one of those dolls which repeats " Mamma " whenever you squeeze it, but he had already turned his back and was striding away, among a staff composed of what seemed to me huge men with wide hats, nodding plumes, tricolour sashes and gilded swords.

Half an hour later I found myself in a small barred cell on the ground floor of the Bishop of Savona's Palace, which had been taken over by General Bonaparte as his headquarters.

§ 3

The first hours or so in that dim, comfortless room were among the most miserable of my existence. I have appeared on more battlefields than you have fingers and toes, my little Suzanne, and I was in the retreat from Moscow, but never have I experienced such a faltering of the spirit as fell upon me at that moment, for hardly had the key turned in the lock when I gave myself up for lost. There was I at the beginning of a military career, a career which I had promised myself and, what was more important, my father and my family, would be great and glorious or would be cut short only by the enemy on the battlefield. And here it was at an end before it had begun. I was under no delusions. The order was strict and was enforced with strictness, and I had been caught in the act, and by the Commander-in-Chief himself. What hope had I? What extenuating circumstances could I plead before the court which would assemble in a few brief hours? As the beams of the morning sun were striking the snows of the Col de Tende I should be lucky, I reflected bitterly, if I escaped the firing squad, and as the moments passed I found myself praying that I should not escape it, for I had lost my honour and I had dragged the name of de Blanchegarde in the dust. Yet even in that moment I mastered my sense of drama. I knew that in fact I should not be condemned to death. Had I fought my man and killed him, ah, that would have been a different thing. Then, indeed, I should have felt my back against a rough stone wall and seen the levelled muskets pointed at my chest. But we had not in fact crossed blades and this circumstance would preserve me from the death penalty. But the least I could hope for was three years with a cannon-ball chained to my right ankle in a convict settlement on the Brittany coast or, worse still, in the hulks of Marseilles harbour. Scarcely, you will agree, a pleasing prospect for a young man on the threshold of a military career.

How long I had been in that room, or rather cell — it contained nothing but a stool and a bundle of not over-clean straw — I do not know, when I saw the hand at the barred window. It was the merest chance that I saw it, for the swift Mediterranean twilight had come and gone, and outside it was dark. The window was high up, above the height of a man's head, and looking upwards at it I could see only the sky still suffused with the afterglow of sunset and pricked with an early star or two. Against it the hand, all four fingers and thumb spread wide, was clearly visible. So it remained an instant, then it gripped the bars and a moment later I saw the pale moon of a face adorned with a pair of huge moustaches. I recognised it at once. Pasquier was outside.

"Comrade," he said in a husky whisper.

I jerked my head and came close to the wall, where I stood looking upwards.

"Yes, Pasquier," I said. "I'm here."

"Listen, son, I've news for you."

"The court-martial—— ? "

"Shut up. I've no time to lose. The court-martial will sit all right, and if you appear before it there's no hope for you. Listen. We've had our orders. We're to send out two patrols at dawn. Our squadron's one of them. Argenteau " — he was the Austrian General opposed to us — " has broken up his cantonments and is on the move. We are to follow his movements. Come on the patrol with us and you'll retrieve everything. It's the chance of a lifetime."

"How the hell am I to get out of here ? " I whispered back.

"Listen," rejoined Pasquier. "I've got Miribel tethered to the fourth plane-tree on the left as you go down the avenue, and as for getting out, have you had supper yet ? "

"No," I answered. "Will they give me supper ? "

"When it comes, use this for seasoning," and as he spoke he thrust something through the bars of the window, which fell with a soft plop on the floor.

"But," I began, "but——" But his face was gone.

I moved away from the wall, and bending down ran my hand over the now invisible floor till I encountered that which he had dropped. It proved to be a small bag, one of those silk bags in which gunners put the powder for the charge, and at first I thought it was in fact filled with that substance. Until I opened it. I put my nose into the bag and sneezed violently. It was filled not with gunpowder, my children, but with pepper, good, strong, well-ground black pepper. Where Pasquier had got it from I neither knew nor cared. As I grasped it I realised at once what he meant by telling me to season my supper.

I withdrew to the pile of straw and waited. My children, it seemed that I waited all night. I grew hungrier and hungrier and more and more impatient. Was I to be left to starve? Was I to face a court-martial fasting? It had long since grown too dark for me to tell the time by my grandfather's watch, and the cell, facing north, was cold, or perhaps it was that my blood was now cool. I only know that from time to time I shivered, and when I did so I could not help thinking of Miribel, my little mare, the pride and joy of my existence, tied up to the fourth plane-tree on the left of the avenue. How was she faring? Was she as cold as her unhappy, incarcerated master?

At last I heard footsteps approaching. They came clumping up to the door, and without a sound I rose from the pile of straw, grasping the bag of pepper in my right hand, and took two paces along the wall of the room. There was a grinding of bolts, a creak of hinges, and a loud hiccup. The door swung slowly open. A dim, bearded figure with a forage cap on its head loomed vaguely between the jambs. Again a loud hiccup rent the dusky air.

" I forgot — hic — all about you," said a vinous voice. " Damn nearly didn't bring your supper. Doesn't matter anyway. This is the last time you——"

But my gaoler did not complete his sentence. As he stood peering vaguely into the gloom of my cell I ran lightly forward on the balls of my feet. With my right hand I flung the contents of the bag full in his face, with my left I dealt him a buffet under the jaw. I cannot tell you, my children, whether the sound he emitted was a hiccup or a sneeze or both, for so appalling was it that, old as I am, it still sometimes echoes in my ears when, after a bottle of your father's Vougeot, I have a nightmare.

I did not stop to examine my gaoler's condition, but snatching the forage cap from his head I rushed from the cell, swung the heavy door to and turned the huge key in the lock. Holding the bunch, of which it formed the principal piece, in my hand, I ran down the corridor, adjusting the forage cap on my head as I did so. It was a poor disguise but it might deceive someone at a distance for a moment. Luck was with me, however. The corridor was empty, so also was the stone hall beyond, across which I ran with the speed of desperation. Its big door was bolted. With feverish hands I tore at the bolts. The key, thank God, was in the lock. As I struggled to turn it I heard a voice.

" Where are you off to, Jules ? "

I was, you understand, in deep shadow and hardly visible.

" Shan't be a moment," I said gruffly. " Nature calls," and I gave a loud hiccup.

At that moment, with a shriek and a squeak the lock

turned. I dragged open the door and in a second found myself outside beneath the stars. Half a moment later I was walking Miribel very slowly, soothing her and stroking her neck beneath the plane-trees, and it was not until I reached the end of the avenue and was at the top of the main street of Savona that I ventured to touch her flanks and break into a canter.

§ 4

Dawn found me once more in the saddle, after an hour or two's troubled sleep covered with a horse blanket in the remains of a barn. When I say dawn that is not quite accurate. It was that brief half-hour before the sun peeps over the horizon, that moment when the world is cold, grey and uncomfortable. But I saw none of these things. All that devoured me like a raging flame was impatience, impatience to be off with the forty-nine other hussars detailed to reconnoitre the position of the Austrians. For the fifth time I fiddled with my right stirrup leather, though I had adjusted it to my satisfaction minutes before. For about the fiftieth time I eased my sabre in its sheath. Yes, my sabre, my children. How Pasquier had got it back from the Gendarmerie — for, of course, they had taken it away from me on my arrest — I did not enquire. Pasquier had performed many miracles since the evening before ; that was one of them. Yet even Pasquier was impatient. I could tell by the way he tugged at his left-hand horn — I mean moustache, twisting the end and tickling his ear with it. If I had attempted to do that with my moustache it would have meant disaster. The wax . . .

At last the lieutenant gave the order : " Walk — March." With a jingle of bits, a cough or two, and an unfortunate noise from Chavasse's sorrel, who always behaved badly at the wrong moment till she bolted with him at Marengo and saved his life, we moved off and I breathed a trifle more easily. If my escape had not already been discovered — and there had been no hue and cry — the court-martial was even now assembling sleepily, and doubtless blasphemously, in a small room in the Bishop's Palace. I could see it in my mind's eye, tall, with a tarnished cornice, and a carved table with chairs round it, and that musty, ecclesiastical smell, the odour of sanctity as your great-aunt Marthe used to call it. Yes, the members would enter grumbling, while the prisoner was five leagues away with Miribel between his knees and the enemy ahead. What's that, Gaston ? Why didn't the officer notice me ? You are an intelligent boy and take after your old grandfather. He didn't notice me, my dear, because I took very good care that he should not. I kept in the foreground, for with Pasquier and several others I formed part of the small advance-guard which, with single scouts out on our flank, formed a protection against surprise for the main body of the patrol. The officer was, of course, with that body, that is to say a good three hundred paces behind us. At that distance it would have been hard for him to recognise me. Moreover, soldiers being all dressed alike, are apt to look alike, and even hussars are no exception to that rule.

I trotted forward with the rest, my eyes on the shoulder of a mountain some five miles away which there ran down into the plain. The country was much cut up by little woods, watercourses, bone dry in the summer but which now held streams in their embrace, and here and there a straggling vineyard. We were following a rough track which led, I was told, eventually to the village of Montenotte on the slopes of Monte Legino. It was there, a few days later, that General Bonaparte astonished and confounded the world with the first of his great victories.

But that morning neither he nor his armies were at the place, only fifty of his hussars moving towards it in battle formation, probing, groping for the Austrians. And none more eager than Armand de Blanchegarde, who knew well enough that his only chance to wipe clean his slate, to rehabilitate himself, was to perform some act of valour on this, his first engagement with the enemy. Yes, my children, I rode forward that day, my mind uneasy but my heart aglow. Men are always keyed up when they go into action for the first time and, whatever they may say, most of them are afraid. I was afraid that morning, I do not mind confessing it. Behind every bush and thicket, every rough-tiled cottage and stable, I expected to see the white coat of an Austrian and the flash of his musket. For me there was a double fear, not only of what the immediate future held for me but of what I had left behind. There had been no mercy in General Bonaparte's eyes, only justice, cold and keen as a sword.

It was full daylight when we reached the inn, having covered perhaps four leagues and seen nothing of the enemy, not even a watch-fire pale against the imminent dawn. It was a large place, the inn, built round three sides of a courtyard, the fourth being occupied by a singularly large and smelly midden. Mine host of the Two Crows — for that was its name — was standing in the stone archway leading to the courtyard. He was a little man with three days' growth of dark beard on his chin and a wart on the left side of his nose. When he smiled, the skin on his face wrinkled like that of a walnut. He was smiling then. Come to think of it, he was always smiling, he never stopped. Not only was he smiling, but he was full of drink and information. No, no Austrians had come near the Two Crows so far, though his son Demetrio had seen six only the evening before, " Hussars like yourselves, signori, tall, very savage men." To Pasquier's question as to where they were, he pointed vaguely to the hills in front and beyond.

" Out there, out there, signori, and they are part, it seems, of a strong Austrian force. They are wicked men, very wicked men. They took old Giacomo and hanged him, and as for Teresa, his daughter . . ." He shrugged eloquent shoulders.

It was at that moment that the officer arrived. His name, Gaston ? Haven't I told you his name ? It was Juvisy, and I didn't know him well, for he had only lately joined us. A dapper little man, he sat his horse well and hardly ever stopped talking. He came clattering up at this moment.

" What's all this, what's all this ? Now then, men, let's have it. Who is in command here ? Who's in command ? "

Pasquier was the eldest soldier present and he explained the situation to the lieutenant. At the mention of a strong force of cavalry some distance ahead — " An hour's ride, Your Excellency, an hour's ride," broke in the little innkeeper, who was even more voluble than Juvisy — I saw the lieutenant's countenance change and his lips tighten.

" Well, on we go," he said, " and this time we'll keep together."

I saw Pasquier's eyebrows go up, and Sergeant Chardin, one of the oldest soldiers of the Regiment and a prominent member of the *Clique*, seemed about to speak. Even I, as a recruit, could see that this was an imprudence. If we were to meet the enemy within the hour, common sense dictated that a scout or two should be thrown out in advance to give the main body early warning of their presence.

It was not for us, however, to question orders, and we all set off, Juvisy at our head. I watched him as we rode along the rough road. He kept turning and twisting in his saddle, dropping his reins and putting his hands first to his side and then to his belly. He had hardly gone five hundred yards, and the inn had only just disappeared from view behind us round a bend of the road, when Juvisy called a halt. His face was contorted. I saw beads of sweat trickling down his forehead beneath his shako.

"I can't go on, I can't go on. I feel very ill," he said, and swayed in his saddle so that I thought he would fall. With a great effort he recovered himself, thrust a hand into the opening of his tunic and drew out a crumpled piece of paper. "The orders," he said. "Sergeant Chardin, you are in command. I must get back to the inn. I'll wait for you there. I'll— I'll——" and his voice died away to a mumble.

Then he turned his horse's head and moved back along the way we had come, towards the Two Crows. We let him go in silence. It was not for us to make any comment and we did not do so. He was hardly out of earshot when Chardin was at my side, thrusting his horse between mine and Pasquier's.

"This is the very devil," he said, clutching the written orders — they were, I perceived, upside down. "What the hell do I do now ? I can't read 'em."

"If you turned them the other way up, Sergeant——" I began.

" Heads up or tails down it's all the same to me," grumbled Chardin. " I can't read them because I can't read. Here, Pasquier."

Pasquier shook his head. " I can't either," he said.

" Can I read them ? " I said, " and shew you our route on the map which I perceive is attached to them ? "

Sergeant Chardin looked at me and slowly shook his head.

" I can't command troops through an interpreter, boy," he answered. " This is a fine business. The only man who can read goes off to the rear with a bellyache."

" The only man who can read ? " I exclaimed.

" How long have you been in the Regiment ? "

" Six weeks."

" Have you ever seen any of us reading ? "

" No," I said.

" Of course you haven't. And why, boy ? Because we can't, none of us. The Hussars of Angers don't read, they fight."

" But if we go forward without using the map——" I began.

" Precisely," he interrupted. " I shall have to use half of you as scouts and that will weaken the main body and we shall do no good."

It was then that Pasquier rose to the occasion. My children, I never thought that a simple soldier could show so much perspicacity, could be so true and accurate a reader of character. But then, of course, he had known me six weeks.

" Let young de Blanchegarde lead us," he said. " He's been to school and, Sacred Blue, he's the son of a General."

The words were hardly out of his mouth when there

was a growl of assent from the dozen or so old soldiers grouped round us.

"Yes, you take the lead, young de Blanchegarde. We'll follow. We'll do what you tell us."

My children, the sun at that moment rose in front of us and peered over Monte Legino. For me he has never shone so brightly again. The whole valley was filled with a golden light which bathed my gallant company in its radiance and warmed my face and my heart. Of all moments in my career, that was the most glorious. I tore my sabre from its sheath. I waved it aloft.

"*En avant*, my comrades," I shouted. "To death or glory."

"Don't be such a goddamn fool. Send out your scouts," growled Chardin.

His words sobered me. In an instant I was no longer the young cavalryman about to charge, but the cool commander with the ice-cold brain. I returned my sabre to its sheath, did as he advised me and so we went forward, moving in a north-easterly direction to where I hoped and expected to encounter the enemy.

We marched for more than two hours before anything happened. Then I saw coming towards me, moving at a slow trot through some dwarf oak-trees, one of our scouts. Running, hopping and panting at his saddle, his hands tied with a bit of rope of which one end was in the hand of the trooper, was a shaggy-haired peasant.

"Caught him up in the wood yonder," said the trooper. "Can't understand what he says."

I questioned this sad-looking individual. I too found it very hard to understand him, but I had learnt enough even by then to watch men's faces when they answer your questions, and it did not take me long to make

27

up my mind that the man was lying. He swore by Saint Chrysostom, Saint Polycarp, Saint John the Evangelist and a number of other saints that he had been in the neighbourhood all that day and the day before, indeed all his life, and had seen no enemy.

" Are you certain that you were in the neighbourhood this morning ? " I barked.

It appeared that he was, and that there was nothing unusual to report. I was convinced that he was lying, that he was, in fact, a paid spy such as the Austrians used in great numbers in Italy, mostly to report about the feelings of the local populace, who were not at all fond of them. He was lying because, if the written orders which I carried and the map did not lie, we were very close to the cantonments of the enemy.

I sat in my saddle gazing at the sullen peasant, and as I did so I remembered some advice my father had given me in the matter of dealing with partisans and unofficial soldiers, if I may so call them. I put my hand to my waxed moustaches and endeavoured to twirl them. It was excruciatingly painful, my children, but it gave to my face what I hope was a fierce expression, though I trust the peasant did not notice that my eyes were watering.

" What ? " I roared. " What, you scum ? You have just come through country occupied by a full corps of the Austrian Army and maintain that you have seen nothing ! You're a spy, that's what you are. Take him away and shoot him."

I jerked my head. Four of my hussars — yes, my children, they were my hussars that day and don't forget it — slipped from their saddles and began ostentatiously loading their carbines. They had seen me wink and knew what I meant. But the peasant had not seen me and he, my children, immediately became a very frightened man. His knees knocked together, his tongue slobbered between his lips, his Adam's apple jerked up and down. He manifested, in fact, all the symptoms of a man stricken with mortal fear.

" Monseigneur," he cried, rushing forward to my saddle till the rope which bound him brought him up short, " I will tell the truth, I swear it, I swear it by Saint Chrysostom, by Saint Polycarp——"

I cut him short with a gesture.

" Spare us the Litany and tell us the truth."

This was his story. He was, it appeared, a groom attached to a convent of monks, of which the prior had sent him on an errand, telling him that if, when performing it, he ran into any Frenchmen he was to warn them immediately that a detachment of the Austrian regiment of the Hussars of Barco were quartered in a little hamlet close by. Here the peasant turned and pointed, and indeed not far away but masked by trees and the shoulder of a mountain I could perceive what I now realised was the glint of the sun upon tiles.

" How are their sentries posted ? " I asked.

The peasant, or rather groom, explained that in the gardens of the houses facing towards the French army a dozen men or more had been posted to form the main guard. They were dismounted and standing on watch behind the high hedges with which the gardens of those houses were surrounded. Here the groom paused.

" And the rest, man, the rest," I said. " Where are the others ? "

" The others, Monseigneur ? I do not think they apprehend danger. When I left them, not a quarter of an hour ago, they were preparing to water their horses at the village pond."

I felt my heart beginning to beat more rapidly.
" And where's that, oaf ? "
" On the other side of the village, sir."

I made my plan in an instant, my children. On my orders the men were formed up in a single body, and one of them took the peasant up behind him. I ordered the man to lead us round the hamlet through the woods which, fortunately for us, spread in abundance on every side so that we could fall upon the Austrians as they were watering their horses. I told the man I would let him go unscathed the moment we caught sight of the enemy. To show him I meant business I myself rode beside him, the muzzle of my pistol jammed into his ribs. Its powers of persuasion were wonderful, for he proved an excellent guide.

High hedges and the skirts of a fair-sized wood masked our approach. We rode right round the village until we found a little copse where we halted. There in silence two hussars gagged the peasant and tied him to a tree. While they were so doing, I was in agony lest someone should make a noise or Chavasse's sorrel forget herself again, for there, not four hundred yards away, were the enemy. They were watering their horses just as the peasant had told us, at the edge of a fair-sized pond. The Austrian troopers were, I noticed, armed, but their officers had forgotten to take a very essential precaution. It was this, my children. When you are close to the enemy, you do not let all your horses drink at one and the same time. You send them troop by troop to the stream — or, in this case, the pond — so that the others can be ready at all times to repel a sudden attack. It was precisely this step which the Austrians had neglected to take. I suppose they thought that their main guard behind the hedges in front of the houses well beyond the pond was sufficient.

It was this that ruined them. As soon as the peasant was secured I passed the word along the ranks to draw sabres, to form into line, to advance at the trot, and, above all, not to raise a shout until we were on them. In a moment we were in motion. I placed myself in the centre of the line, twenty yards ahead of it, and so with a rasp of steel and a jingle of bits we broke into a trot. My children, how can I describe that day? Fifty years and more have passed but I remember it as if it were yesterday. The bright Italian sun shone down upon me, glinting upon my flashing sabre. I was not yet eighteen, I had a good horse between my knees, before me was the enemy and behind, stout-hearted comrades, forty-eight of them, and we were bearing down upon the foe.

Forgetting my own orders, I clapped spurs to Miribel who broke at once into a full gallop, and let out a bloodcurdling yell. No, Gaston, it was not " *Vive l'Empereur !* " It was before the days of the Empire. Bonaparte, as I have told you, was only a General then. I shouted " *Vive la Révolution !* " The rest echoed the shout and onwards we thundered. It seemed but a moment before I reached the banks of the pond. They were steep, too steep for horses standing in the pond or at its edge to climb them, and the only practical way down to the water was a roughly levelled opening in the banks. It was for this opening that I made, for it was jammed choc-a-bloc with Austrian troopers either leading their horses to the water or away from it after they had drunk their fill.

In an instant we were among them, hacking and hewing. The air was full of shouts and cries, and a sharp, sour smell. We were through them in less time than it takes me to tell this story, and I saw as I came up the other side that the point of my sabre was red, — I do not remember how it came to be so. Half the Austrians were down. The pop-pop of carbines showed that Sergeant Chardin and some of his men had halted and were shooting down the Hussars of Barco where they still struggled desperately in the muddy and now bloody pond. About thirty of them, however, were still capable of fight. They were about a hundred yards away, and a great brute of a man with a grey moustache and a captain's insignia was yelling at them, tugging at the bridle of a black horse. The Hussars of Barco are fine soldiers, I must concede them that. Surprised though they had been and half cut to pieces, yet that captain had rallied the remnant. They were on a sort of island on the south side of the pond, a submerged island, you understand, for the water came up to just above the hocks of their horses. At that instant reinforcements appeared for them in the shape of the main guard, whom I perceived running hastily from the shelter of the houses which formed the background of the encounter. There was not an instant to lose.

" *En avant*, comrades," I shouted. " Charge ! " and I spurred Miribel into the pond, making straight for the huge Austrian captain. He was a giant, my children. His eyes flashed flame, his sabre was ten feet long. He aimed a blow at my head. I had raised my own sabre to parry it, when, with a flash of intuition, I realised that, if the blades met, mine would be inevitably beaten down. At the ultimate moment therefore I ducked, thrust my body out along Miribel's neck, and took the Austrian in the throat with my point. His sabre fell on my shoulder. It cut through my tunic, pierced the skin and jarred but did not break the bone, for it was a blow

32

delivered by a dying man and the strength had already passed from it.

The death of the Austrian captain was the signal for the end of the fight. All round me Austrians were throwing down their arms and surrendering in a queer jargon of incomprehensible tongues. Sergeant Chardin had dismounted and was methodically accepting their sabres, bundling them under his left arm like so many sticks. A clatter of hoofs faintly heard beyond the village showed where the few who had escaped were making good their retreat. It was the sound of their hoofs which roused me to consider the position.

Here was I, at least three hours away from our main army, in contact with the Austrians whose main body must inevitably be close at hand. Retreat was both prudent and necessary, for the little victory I had scored would, if we stayed, be turned into a little defeat and the victors be vanquished. Already Pasquier was bellowing to the men to re-form. In five minutes we were off again back towards the inn of the Two Crows, leaving behind us four of our own number killed. With us went half a dozen wounded, including Chavasse, bleeding but still capable of sitting their horses. With us, too, I took seventeen mounted Austrians. All were unwounded, all were sullen, all were our prisoners. Here was my proof of victory.

We paused a moment at the top of a hillock to make better arrangements to secure our prisoners on the march and to bind up the wounds of our casualties. Looking back, I saw a sight, my children, which filled me with pride. Those few of the Hussars of Barco who had escaped our charge had roused a hornets' nest. There on the hillside, three miles beyond the village, I could see several white-coated columns — four, to be

33

exact. They were moving forward very slowly, and between them I caught the glint of cannon, and in front of them the flash of sabres and of the points of lances. The Austrians were advancing in force, advancing against us, fifty Hussars of Angers. They were doing it at a snail's pace. My bosom swelled with pride as I turned away. I had provoked an army corps.

I dispatched Pasquier and two other men on the three best of the captured Austrian horses, which were far fresher than ours, with orders to gallop to Savona and inform General Headquarters of the whereabouts of the enemy and of the results of our skirmish.

We returned to the Two Crows at a slow trot. I will not tell you of the things that the Hussars of Angers said to me on the way there, but one phrase I will repeat, and no praise that I have ever had, not even from the Emperor himself, has ever sounded so sweet in my ears. " Boy," said old Chardin, " you are now truly of the Hussars of Angers, and, what is more, of the *Clique*." And there and then he cut the coveted gash on the top right-hand button of my tunic.

At the inn door I was again met by the little innkeeper. His face was wreathed in smiles, and he continued to smile while informing me that Lieutenant Juvisy was, he thought, very sick, for he had knocked upon the door of his room and received no reply. " It may be," added the little innkeeper, " that it is something he has eaten."

I was in no mood to knock at the door of invalids, my children. I confess I forgot my manners and thrust it open. There indeed was Juvisy and I comprehended at once the meaning of the innkeeper's remark. He was sprawled across a truckle bed. In his hand was a bottle, its mouth pointing to the floor. On a table by his side was the skeleton of a goose, a few crusts of bread, and a large bowl which had once contained, so the innkeeper informed me later, three pounds of dried apricots.

I was regarding this scene and listening to the snores of poor sick Juvisy when there came a clatter of footsteps behind me. One of the hussars entered and saluted — yes, my children, he saluted me, the same rank as himself.

" General's outside. Wants you at once."

I turned, left the room and a moment later found myself in the bright sunshine of the courtyard. My exultation was leaving me. I should have to explain myself to the ferocious Macard, him, you will remember, who was accustomed to fight the enemy stripped to the waist.

But it was not General Macard who stood there waiting for me, and the exultation ebbed altogether, for there in his stead was a little short man in a white-and-blue coat, with a sallow skin and quiet, piercing eyes. Behind him were three or four tall Generals with nodding plumes and tricolour sashes. I saluted and stood to attention. General Bonaparte looked me up and down.

" How many of the enemy do you estimate you saw after your skirmish, hussar ? " His tone was like a whiplash.

" I counted four columns, *mon général*, composed, I should estimate, of not less than four battalions each."

" God's breath, the whole of Argenteau's advance-guard," said the tall Augereau, who was one day to be my chief. He was a pace behind the General. Bonaparte made a quick, irritable gesture with his hand.

" How far distant ? "

" Two hours' march, *mon général*. But——" I paused.

" But what ? " snapped Bonaparte.

" I do not think they will be here in two hours, sir. They were moving very slowly when I last saw them."

" Why was that ? "

I drew myself up, my children, and out of the corner of my eye I could see my men all standing stiff as I was, and old Chardin with his bundle of sabres sticking out from his arm.

" Because they have encountered the Hussars of Angers."

Bonaparte's eye raked me. I swear, my children, that when I charged the sixteen-gun battery at Wagram it was a lesser moment. Then he stepped forward. I felt a tingling sensation in my ear. Yes, my children, he had pulled me by the ear, a gesture which was soon to be famous throughout France, throughout the Grande Armée, throughout the Empire.

" Be ready to take out another patrol in an hour's time, lieutenant," he said.

What's that, Suzanne ? Yes, he promoted me there and then — on the field of battle you might say — or only just off it. The court-martial ? I never heard another word about that. Yes, I did take out another patrol, but we saw nothing at all. A bit of luck in the morning, no luck at all in the afternoon, that is the way of war. No, no, not tonight. It is long past bedtime. You must wait until tomorrow.

The Intercepted Dispatch

§ 1

MUD, my little Suzanne, you call that mud ? — Those few little spots of brown on the hem of your skirt where you were splashed this afternoon by the phaeton of Monsieur de Brissac. There is nothing I do not know about it, my dear. If you care to listen to an old man's stories, I can tell you something about mud — hundreds of leagues of it which cost the Emperor thirty thousand men.

Yes, Gaston, my lad, you may pour me out a glass of sherry. I have seen great casks of it standing on the quays along the Guadalquivir in the Spanish sunshine, and I would have been glad of a barrel or two of it in the winter of 1806 in the marshes of Poland. That, if you like, was a campaign ! all mud, as aforesaid, and rain, with spells, in between, of snow and frost. The Emperor himself said that in Poland he had discovered a new element. And all we had to hearten us was watery beer and very little of that. Why, I remember that King Joachim Murat himself, or the Grand Duke of Berg as he was then, received a bottle of thin wine and a loaf of bread from Lasalle on Christmas Day, 1806, as a present, and was thankful to get it.

To understand what I am going to tell you, you must get the kind of country fixed in your mind. Poland is a huge plain, cut up by rivers and forests and marshes, the most God-forsaken country in the world. The plains consist of sand, swamp and water, and there are more dykes, forests, lakes and morasses than I should

37

have thought existed anywhere. There were no paved roads — merely banks of earth. In December 1806 the infantry sank to their knees and often further in that soft stuff. They used cords to bind their boots, or what was left of them, to their feet, and I once saw a whole battalion, each man pulling his rear leg out of the slough, like a carrot, with both hands, his musket slung across his shoulders.

The main road from Posen to Warsaw was like that, and the bridges across the frequent streams were made of undressed logs of wood on which the carriages bumped and crashed, and frequently overturned. Grand Marshal Duroc himself broke his collar-bone when his carriage was upset on that same road. The horses sank into the mud up to their hocks and the guns to their axles, a league and a half an hour was the maximum pace for infantry and cavalry alike and a march of ten leagues was a long day's business.

That was the sort of country into which the Emperor had led us to fight the Russians, the one people in Europe, except always the mad English, who in 1806 still dared to defy him. He had taught the Prussians their lesson that year at Jena and Auerstadt. But the Russians were a different proposition. Up to that time we had not had much to do with them, though their Imperial Guard had received something at Austerlitz that they were likely to remember. Now, however, they were alone, except for Lestocq's Prussian corps, and under their General Bennigsen they had given us a certain amount of trouble.

In those days I was on Augereau's staff — it was before I was transferred to Lannes — and I had "stopped one" at Golymin where we arrived rather late to support Davout. It was nothing much, a graze from a musket ball which I caught when I was in Rapp's charge with his dragoons. The Russian light troops took us in flank, their men standing waist-deep in a marsh and giving us several volleys as we passed. The wound, as I have said, was nothing much, but it laid me up for some time, and it was not until the 31st of January 1807 that I caught up with the Army again, for I had gone back to Warsaw, you understand, to recover.

To comprehend what follows you must take a lesson in strategy. You see, on this old map, the position of the two Armies and what each was trying to do. Here is Mohrungen, which had been occupied by the Russian commander on the 26th. He had pushed his advance-guard under Bagration as far as Liebemühl on the right and Allenstein on the left, and Allenstein had been evacuated by Marshal Bernadotte, who had marched on Lobau. Bennigsen had a grand plan which was nothing less than to drive Napoleon and the whole of the Grande Armée back across the Vistula. To achieve it, he had made a great march against our left with the object of separating it from the main body, thus forcing the Emperor to retreat. A capital plan, if he had been dealing with a general of ordinary capacity. But he was fighting Napoleon and the Emperor had devised a counter-scheme for his complete destruction. The corps of Bernadotte was to retreat slowly and doggedly towards Thorn and the Vistula and entice the Russians in pursuit till they were caught by the wings of the Grande Armée as in the grip of a pair of pincers. Bennigsen, you understand, was to move forward blindly, full of the notion that he was lopping off our left wing like the branch of a tree from its trunk, whereas that branch was in fact stiffening and curling round to

39

join the trunk higher up, thus enclosing the Russian Army in a circle from which there would be no escape.

Now in that country one of the main difficulties faced by the officers of the staff, more especially the aides-de-camp, was the quick transmission of orders. So heavy were the roads that it might be a matter of days to carry a dispatch from headquarters to the corps concerned. Headquarters, moreover, were constantly changing as the Army moved forward or back. To give you an idea of the difficulty, I may tell you that my friend De Feznesac, who was of Ney's staff, took four days and lost two horses in moving from the advance-guard to general headquarters, a distance of not more than fifty leagues. It was not surprising therefore that the supply of aides-de-camp and orderly officers only too often fell short of requirements. The dispatches were often late and sometimes went astray. We who were on the staff led a dog's life and had often to see our work, for lack of sufficient staff officers, entrusted to other men. The practice — and it was a practice of which I strongly disapproved — was for any officer who happened to be joining his corps from the rear and passing anywhere near headquarters to report himself before proceeding, so that, if by any chance the Emperor desired to send a dispatch to a particular corps commander, he could use the services of an officer joining that corps and thus effect a saving both in time and men. That was the theory, you understand. But it was a dangerous system and in practice was bound to break down sooner or later. On the one hand, you had a number of trained staff officers like myself who knew the lie of the country and something of the field of operations. On such men it was possible to rely. On the other hand, you had any Tom, Dick or Harry from

St. Cyr — transport officers, artillerymen, anyone you please — all streaming forward from the rear to join their units. Not infrequently dispatches of the greatest importance were handed to one of these men simply because he happened to be going in the desired direction. The fact that we were driven to such methods is itself a proof of the appalling difficulties of that campaign.

The whole army was, in fact, disorganised. We left Germany one hundred and forty thousand strong, but we numbered scarcely eighty thousand when we caught the Russians at Eylau, so you can realise how great was the number of stragglers. I do not see how it could have been avoided, for that was no country for weaklings. Anyone who was not absolutely fit and strong had to be left behind and his chances of survival were pretty small, once he fell out of the ranks.

§ 2

I reached Willenburg, where the Emperor had his headquarters, on the 31st of January. My journey thither from Warsaw is more easily imagined than described. My wound was more or less healed. It was, as I say, only a scratch, a flesh wound in the left shoulder. But I had had nothing but two potatoes and an onion for forty-eight hours and a glass of what they called beer, which tasted like stagnant water. Everywhere along those appalling roads I met parties of stragglers and other riff-raff that always hang on to the skirts of a great army and do more harm in five minutes than disciplined troops in a month.

I reported at once to headquarters on my arrival, where, to my great content, I was told to proceed immediately to join Marshal Augereau. I was informed that he was either at Neidenburg or at Janow, that was to say more or less in the centre of our right wing. At that time I had no very clear idea of the general plan. All I knew was that we had been in touch with the Russians a few days earlier, that Bernadotte was falling back in accordance with orders, and that the Emperor expected to win a great victory within four days at most. You will understand, therefore, my eagerness to get back to the front, for you don't get promotion in the rear, or rather you didn't in those days. Later on it was different.

I accordingly pushed out from Willenburg about one in the afternoon, on my black charger, Aigle — a fine horse that had served me well throughout the Jena campaign. If I was cold and hungry, so was he ; though I had found a little fodder for him that morning, the first he had had for twenty-four hours. He turned his head as I prepared to mount him outside the only large house in the filthy street where the Emperor had his headquarters, and the look in his eye meant plainly enough : " I am fed up with this country and this weather."

I clapped him on the shoulder as I hoisted myself into the saddle.

" It's the fortune of war, old man," I said to him.

So off we started in an icy drizzle which turned, later on, to snow, as sorry a couple as you could well find. Do not imagine, my dear, that the Emperor's campaigns always looked like those pictures they have put up at Versailles. You see, perhaps, your grandfather wearing a spotless uniform, with flying dolman and a plumed shako all complete, mounted on a black horse and proceeding at full gallop across the landscape, with the enemy showing as a straggling row of backs in the top corner. War, my children, is seldom like that. My uniform was far from spotless. I was soaked to the skin. There was no plume to my shako. My horse had not been properly groomed for a week, and, though he still had four shoes on his feet, I expected at any moment that he would lose at least two of them. The mud came half-way up to his hocks at every step we took, and we averaged, I suppose, two leagues an hour.

Thus we proceeded, along a muddy track, for I cannot call it a road, and across a wilderness of dirty plain with a marsh on one side and a dark, inhospitable forest on the other. I was not alone. Small *pelotons* of stragglers were following the same road as myself in a state of the utmost misery. They had left their cantonments scarcely ten days before, but already they looked like old men, with their sunken eyes, their lank cheeks and bristles on their chins.

I had seen the Emperor for a moment when I had reported myself. He had been moving about among his Guard, quiet, calm as he always was when things were not going well, but these stragglers had no regard for the Emperor. Most of them were sullen, the others were cursing. Not a few fell out, too exhausted to go further, whereupon they were instantly stripped by the horde of filthy camp followers that seemed to spring from nowhere the moment a soldier gave up the struggle.

§ 3

I had been going, I suppose, three hours on this journey when I first encountered Monsieur de la Tour de Grandchamps. He was a young officer, the hair scarcely visible on his upper lip. When I came up with him he was sitting by the roadside, dismally regarding what I suppose he would have called a horse, though it looked to me like an animated skeleton, and not so very animated at that. Its head hung down to its knees. It was standing stock-still, except for small shudders that passed now and then across its withers. The young fellow was wearing a brand-new uniform that showed him to belong to the Ninth Hussars. I do not know why, for I had passed a hundred such, mostly on foot, since I had started, but I drew rein when I saw him. There was a wistful look in his eye, I think, which made me do so. He seemed so young, so forlorn in the midst of that howling wilderness. A few yards to the left of us lay a corpse, naked except for his trousers — some poor devil of a foot-slogger who had failed to stay the course.

" Are you bound for Neidenburg ? " I asked by way of greeting.

He shook his head.

" No, Monsieur," he answered. " My regiment belongs to the corps of Marshal Bernadotte. I am on the way to His Excellency's headquarters, which I understand are at Strassburg."

He was not, of course, alluding to that pleasant city on the Rhine, but a filthy little town on the river Drewenz.

I raised my eyebrows at that, for he had more than twice the distance to go that I had, and it was obvious to me that darkness would fall long before he reached his destination.

" Our roads lie together," I said, " as far as Neidenburg, where I hope to find Marshal Augereau. From there your best road is through Soldau and Lautenberg. We will journey together, if you will, though your horse looks in an even worse case than mine."

His face brightened at my offer, but he seemed to

feel it was not becoming in a soldier to stand in need of company. He was still, as I have said, very young.

" It's not a bad horse," he said sullenly, " and come to that yours is not as fresh as it might be."

" They might both, as you say, be better," I agreed. " My name is de Blanchegarde," I added casually. " Captain de Blanchegarde. To whom have I the honour of speaking ? "

He told me his name with a spiritless air and suddenly I saw what was the matter with him. He was in the last stages of fatigue. Only his youth had kept him in the saddle.

" This is your first campaign," I said, as he mounted his horse and induced it with savage spurring to shamble forward beside my own.

" What of it ? " he answered roughly. " We all have to start sometime, I suppose."

I forbore to take offence. One does not quarrel with children.

" For all that," he went on with a sudden lift of the head, " I am carrying dispatches, and, if my horse should prove to be the faster, I shall have to leave you, sir."

I raised my eyebrows at that, as we went slowly on knee to knee. I looked him up and down. Heavens, but he was raw — from the crown of his dripping shako to the soles of his new Hessians. He was wearing, I remember, a pair of those large riding-breeches of exaggerated cut, which set off the figure well enough on a horse, but are ludicrous in any other position.

" Dispatches," I said. " To your Colonel, I suppose ? "

He flushed at my remark and gave me a petulant look.

" Not at all," he answered. " Prince Berthier gave

them to me himself. They are from the Emperor to the Prince of Pontecorvo."

" To Bernadotte ? " I asked.

He nodded.

" He gave me to understand that they were of the utmost importance," he said, throwing a chest as he spoke, and digging his spurs once more into his wretched mount.

Perhaps I was not sufficiently impressed. He may even have seen that I was trying hard not to smile at him. His face grew dark with anger.

" You do not believe me," he said. " But it is true, Monsieur, though I fear this is hardly the time or place to convince you."

He touched his sabre hilt as he spoke.

He shewed some spirit, and I felt sorry for the lad. He was obviously bewildered at the pass in which he found himself, and desperately tired with the hardships of the road.

" Of course," I murmured soothingly.

I felt that soon, however, I might have to be severe with him. A soldier who had fought for the Emperor since Montenotte did not require to learn the value of dispatches.

He misunderstood my kindness.

" I perceive, sir," he said, " that you still doubt the importance of my mission."

He thrust his hand, as he spoke, into his tunic and pulled out a document.

" See for yourself," he said, and clapped the dispatch into my hands.

It consisted of a single bit of paper, folded and sealed. But the seal was broken.

" Sir," I said sternly, as I took the document, " do

you observe the condition of this seal ? "

" That is how I received it," he answered shortly.
" I did not break the seal. It was handed to me like
that."

§ 4

To this day I do not quite know what induced me to
read the dispatch. It was no business of mine but the
whole thing was most irregular. Why had Marshal
Berthier entrusted this dispatch to a callow youth fresh
from St. Cyr instead of giving it to a trained aide-de-
camp ? I could not believe that it could be of real
importance. Otherwise there must have been some
pretty bad staff work somewhere.

I unfolded the paper and read. I read it with
attention. I read it a second time with amazement. I
could scarcely believe my eyes. I had doubted whether
the dispatch could be important. My children, it was
vital. It would make all the difference between the
success or failure of the whole of that plan of the Emperor which I have described to you. And here it was —
this vital paper — going to its destination under a broken
seal in the charge of a green youth who was scarcely good
for another ten leagues and riding a horse which would
be falling under him within the next half-hour. I have
thought of the affair often since that day, but have never
been able to find an adequate excuse for Berthier. His
staff work was obviously all to pieces, and at headquarters they must have been simply living from hand
to mouth at that stage of the campaign.

After nearly fifty years I cannot remember the exact
wording of the dispatch, but it was to the effect that the
first corps, commanded by Marshal Bernadotte, was to
join the left of the Army under the immediate command

of the Emperor. This meant another retirement and the march of the corps was to be concealed by being made at midnight, a cavalry regiment remaining behind to burn bivouac fires all night. The Prince of Pontecorvo was to retreat, if possible, to Gilgenburg, but, if necessary, he could still continue to cover the bridgehead of Thorn. Then came details of the position of Soult on the right and Lefebvre on the left. But it was the concluding words of the dispatch which riveted my attention :

" It is unnecessary," wrote Berthier, " for me to tell you that the Emperor intends to destroy the enemy. He directs you therefore to join his left. This movement will strengthen one of the ' pincers ' by which he hopes to effect his purpose. The other ' pincer ' under Lefebvre, who will be supported by Marshal Ney, should be in position within thirty hours. It is of the utmost importance that you should begin to move without delay. The Emperor trusts to your zeal and your knowledge of the circumstances. You will begin your retreat on Gilgenburg not later than tonight."

I looked at the head of the dispatch. It was dated that morning, the 31st of January.

I handed it back to my companion.

" It is, as you say, of the utmost importance," I said. " It is not too much to say that the success of the campaign depends on your placing that dispatch in the hands of Marshal Bernadotte before this evening."

He looked surprised at that, and muttered something about being determined to do his best.

" Understand, sir," said I, " that there can be no question of failure in this case. You perhaps do not fully realise the meaning of the paper you carry. The Emperor has seen fit to entrust the whole plan of his campaign into your keeping. If that paper falls into the enemy's hands, it may cost him thirty thousand men."

"It shall not be seen by the enemy, sir," he answered; "not while I live."

He lifted his head as he spoke, and his eyes flashed. He was a game youngster, but I was in two minds whether I ought not to take the dispatch from him and bear it myself. Then I reflected that, after all, he had as good a chance of delivering it in safety as I had. Neither of us, under the conditions in which we found ourselves, should be carrying such a message at all. Berthier was trusting too much to the zeal and good fortune of a single officer.

We jogged along in silence for some moments, and then he turned to me timidly.

"The Prince of Pontecorvo is ordered to retreat," he said. "I confess, sir, that I am at a loss to understand the Emperor's move."

"What did they teach you at St. Cyr?" I answered.

He began to tell me, eager babe that he was and very anxious to shew that he knew a thing or two. He told me of the various courses through which he had passed; how the best time to charge foot with cavalry was before it had time to form square and while it was engaged with hostile infantry, as though I had been an old man in an armchair instead of having seen my first battle before I was eighteen. I cut him short.

"That is all very well," I said. "But did they teach you how to sum up the lie of the country, how to tell at a glance the number of squadrons in a hostile cavalry force and the number of infantry in support from the glint of the sun on their bayonets? Can you calculate the amount of time in wet weather a corps of all arms will take to move ten leagues?"

" Those are matters of experience, sir," he replied. " In time I trust to learn."

" When you have done so," I answered, " you will realise the value of that dispatch. The Emperor is drawing the Russians into a trap. Bernadotte is to retreat slowly and methodically, and Bennigsen will rush in pursuit of him. The further he advances, the more impossible will it be for him to turn back. Then the pincers will close and Bennigsen will be within their grip. If, however, Bennigsen stays and fights where he is, the pincers will not have time to develop and Bennigsen may be able to turn on our left wing and cut it off."

He nodded.

" It is a pity," he said, " that my horse is so jaded. I have forty leagues to go before I reach Strassburg."

I looked at his mount. The beast was almost at the point of exhaustion. There was nothing else for it. The Emperor's dispatches were of more importance than a horse. I drew rein.

" Halt, sir," I said. " My horse is tired, but in better condition than yours. Take it and push on as quickly as you can."

He hesitated to accept my offer, but I insisted and at last ordered him to make the exchange. It was now, I suppose, about three in the afternoon and the sun was already low. It is quite dark in Poland at four o'clock in the winter.

§ 5

The exchange was made and, wishing him godspeed, I watched him ride away. I could see that even on my horse M. de la Tour de Grandchamps did not make great progress, for he was never more than a few hundred yards ahead. To add to his difficulties snow began to fall and the air grew colder, so that hands and feet became numb and lost all feeling. So spent was the nag I was riding that I was in two minds whether it would not be quicker to proceed on foot. I did not do so, however, but continued on my way, too cold to care much, and thinking only of the moment when I should meet with some of the rear-guard of Augereau. The sun was setting to our right ; the whirling snow ceased a moment and the plain was lit with dying beams from the west. To our left was one of those treacherous places, half forest and half marsh, in which Poland abounds. I could see my late companion a quarter of a mile ahead, a hundred yards or so from the wood. He was plodding steadily on, and, even as I watched him, I saw that he had succeeded in getting Aigle to trot. Then the snow came down again and blotted him out, as though a curtain had fallen. Breathing on my numbed fingers, I continued to move forward, and presently I fell into a kind of dream or doze, in which memories of past battles and skirmishes came into my mind, till I could scarcely distinguish the true from the false. I seemed to see again the sun-drenched plains of Marengo, the turbid Bormida, and Zach's white-coats breaking in confusion before the sabres of Kellermann's cuirassiers.

I returned to myself abruptly. There came the sound of a shot in front of me and a little to the left, followed rapidly by another. I was instantly alert. I put my hand on my sabre, half drawing it from its sheath. There came no further sound for some moments. Then I heard another shot and, after that, a faint cry.

I quickened my spent beast to something like a slow walk. I peered through the snow, and then stopped abruptly. Through the snowy air, half a dozen wiry little men, with long lances and bestriding rough ponies, came rushing at me.

" Cossacks ! " I said to myself.

In a moment I was surrounded ; three lances were at my breast.

If this were the romantic story of a hero, I suppose I should have drawn my sabre ; taken them on all three ; and, charging with a shout of " *Vive l'Empereur !* " split the nearest Cossack to the chin. In actual fact my horse collapsed under me. The lance of one of the Cossacks knocked my shako over my left eye as I came down and, a moment later, I found myself securely held by two of the men, while a resplendent fellow in a black uniform with a sort of fur turban on his head and red boots to his knees with long tassels flopping from them was standing in front of me telling me in excellent French to surrender.

My children, there was nothing else to do. They were six or seven to one, and I was a prisoner. The invitation to surrender was, in fact, only a polite way of asking whether I preferred to have my throat cut then and there, or to come along with them peaceably.

I had realised of course who they were. Bennigsen, in his swift advance on Bernadotte, had flung his cavalry into action well in advance of his infantry. Platow's Cossacks were therefore swarming all over the place and were often to be found between the scattered corps of the Grande Armée. Some of our stragglers had been cut up by them, and doubtless our hussars and chasseurs were similarly at work within the Russian lines. In a war of movement, you understand, such surprises are inevitable.

" I surrender," I answered, and, so saying, I moved

away from my fallen horse, which lay kicking feebly in the snow.

At a sign from the officer, one of the Cossacks dismounted and, pointing to his horse, made me understand that I should get upon it. This I did, whereupon the Cossack, with extreme agility, jumped up behind me, putting his arms round my waist and holding the reins. We then moved off towards the wood which I had noticed some time previously, the Cossack officer riding at my side. They were a wild lot, those Cossacks — it was my first encounter with them — short men, with slitty eyes and yellow faces, very well mounted and wonderfully dexterous with their lances.

"You won't have to ride double for long," said the officer, as we moved forward. "The rest of my command is just ahead of us, and there is a spare horse which a few moments ago belonged to one of your compatriots."

"Indeed, Monsieur," I answered.

He nodded.

"We met him ten minutes before we caught you," he continued. "He put up a bit of a fight and I fear my men have handled him somewhat roughly."

I scarcely heard what he was saying, thinking only of what I should be seeing in a moment and of what it must mean for the Emperor.

We topped a small rise and there, fifty yards away from us, was another body of horsemen, their long lances standing up like saplings against the background of snow. In their midst was a dark patch on the ground. We rode forward and, a moment later, I saw my late companion. His face was towards the sky, white as the snow around it, and from his breast ran a stream of blood where he had been transfixed by a lance.

The Cossack and I slipped from the pony and I moved forward. As I bent over him his eyelids fluttered a moment and then were still. His eyes grew fixed and glassy. He made a slight gesture with his right hand, his fingers curling and uncurling twice. That was all.

A harsh voice, speaking in an unintelligible tongue, sounded in my ear. I turned my head. Some sort of Russian sergeant or corporal — I do not know what their ranks are in the Cossacks — was speaking to the officer in charge of the troop. I did not know what he said, for I could not understand Russian, but I saw well enough what he held in his hand. It was a piece of paper spattered with blood. The seal was broken. The vital dispatch from Marshal Bernadotte had fallen into the hands of the enemy.

My only hope was that the Cossack officer might not realise the importance of his capture. From what we had heard in the French Army, the Cossacks were little better than savages, and their allies, the Bashkirs, who fought with bows and arrows, were the subject of unceasing mirth among our soldiers. Cupids, we called them, and pretty hairy ones they were, too.

But the Cossack officer was no fool. He took the dispatch, and read it. His eye brightened as he thrust it into his sheepskin coat. Then he gave a series of sharp orders, with the result that I found myself one of a party of four riding at a brisk canter, for the ground was a little better here, after the remainder of the Cossacks, who, in charge of their officer, were moving rapidly away in the darkness towards headquarters.

The dispatch would be in the hands of Bennigsen in a few hours.

We proceeded in this manner for a few hundred yards, when the officer and the Cossacks in front of us halted and waited for us to join them.

The officer turned to me.

"I am sorry, sir," he said, "but circumstances compel me to abandon you to my sergeant. I have, however, given him strict instructions to see to your comfort. You will find that we Russians are not unused to the polite customs of war."

I thought rapidly. Could I by any means detain him?

"It is not usual," I began, "in our Army to leave a captive officer in charge of troopers."

"I know that," he answered apologetically, "but the circumstances permit of no other solution. The paper we were fortunate enough to find on your late companion must reach Mohrungen without delay. I halted only to reassure you and to see that you are suitably mounted."

He turned to the Russian sergeant as he spoke, said a few words to him in his own tongue, and the next instant one of the Cossacks led forward my own horse, Aigle. I noticed with pleasure that in the short interval between the death of Monsieur de la Tour de Grand-champs and my capture they had given him a feed from the bags of fodder they carried on their saddle-bows. He looked much fresher than when I had seen him last. I dismounted from the little Cossack pony which I had been bestriding and climbed on to the back of Aigle. The Cossack officer nodded, waved his hand and moved off without another word.

§ 6

The escort in charge of me was now reduced to four including the sergeant. The remaining Cossacks had gone forward with their officer. Evidently he was determined to take no risks, for which I applauded him. He would see to it that the intercepted dispatch reached Russian headquarters in safety.

I will not bother you with my thoughts as I rode over the snow with my captors. I was cold, hungry and miserably wet. But all that was as nothing compared with my mental distress. The Emperor's great plan would be brought to naught. No doubt he would construct a new one, but that was no comfort at the moment. The Emperor, you understand, started on his campaigns with no more than a general idea. He did not follow hard and fast rules like the stupid Austrians, but met each turn of events with some fresh and ingenious scheme of his own. Nevertheless, it was obvious that his present plan would have given him certain victory within the space of four days, perhaps less. That plan had fallen, or would shortly fall, into the hands of General Bennigsen. A new scheme would have to be made and weeks might elapse before the Russians were once more cornered.

All this and more went round and about in my head as we jogged slowly along. My escort, I observed, did not seem to be in any hurry. Presumably they had been in the saddle the best part of twenty-four hours and were as weary as I was. Our slow progress was maddening to a brain tormented with the thought of what I might be doing, as a free man, to remedy, or at least to mitigate, the calamity in which I had become involved. For I realised that, even now, something might be done. I had got more or less fixed in my head the various villages and towns occupied by both armies. Bernadotte, on whose movements the Emperor depended for the success of his plan, was at Strassburg, so Monsieur de la Tour de Grandchamps had informed me. Bennigsen, the Russian General, on the other hand, was at Mohrungen. I and my escort were now somewhere between Willenburg and Neidenburg. The distance from where the Russian officer had parted from me on his mission to Bennigsen in Mohrungen was, if I remembered rightly, somewhat longer than the distance separating me from Marshal Bernadotte's headquarters at Strassburg. The Cossack, moreover, would be moving through country over which our advance-guard was loosely spread and would thus be exposed to a continual risk of capture. A French officer proceeding to Strassburg, on the other hand, would be passing through Augereau's corps. He would be in safety and could move faster. There was still time to save the Emperor's plan or, at any rate, part of it, if only I could escape and reach Bernadotte even an hour before Bennigsen received the Emperor's dispatch. Bernadotte could in that case immediately start his movements. The Russian troops opposing him would be bound to move forward against him, and might well become too far involved to withdraw before Bennigsen had read the captured dispatch and issued the necessary orders for retreat.

In a word, all might yet be saved if only I could reach Bernadotte in time.

I pulled out my watch and in the last light of that brutal winter's day I made out that it was four o'clock in the afternoon. My fingers, as I took out the watch, came into contact with a little phial the existence of which I had momentarily forgotten. It was a bottle containing a solution of opium, which I carried with me, as did more than one of us who did not desire to lie mortally wounded for hours on a battlefield. You put

it to your lips, you understand; drank, and in a few
minutes all was over.

I glanced to the left and right. The Cossack sergeant
was riding a yard or two on my left hand. Of his three
men, two were immediately in front and the other
slightly in the rear to my right. The sergeant, I noted,
was eyeing my watch with an interest which he was
unable to conceal. I looked him in the face and, smiling
weakly, dangled the watch from its chain. It was a good
watch, given me by a girl in Frankfurt a month or two
previously. The Cossack stretched out a hairy palm,
and, still smiling, I handed him the watch. His little
Tartar eyes were gleaming. He held it to his ear,
evidently delighted by its loud tick. He bit the gold
case with his teeth.

" It is a splendid watch," I said to him in French.
" I pray you to keep it."

Of course, he did not understand what I said, but
my gestures made it clear. His companions, who had
been regarding their superior with curiosity, pushed up
and gazed greedily at the watch. It was passed from
hand to hand. Seldom had they seen anything like it.
You must realise that these men were savages. They
could neither read nor write, and to them a watch was
something miraculous, something of which they had
heard but had probably never seen.

Having thus absorbed their attention, I proceeded
to the next move. I took out my flask. It was my most
precious possession, full almost to the brim of burnt
Strassburg brandy of double strength, my last reserve
against the cold, and up to that moment most sparingly
used. Keeping my hands as low as possible, and hitching
forward my dolman to hide what I was doing, I unscrewed
the cap of the flask and, with some little difficulty,

succeeded in emptying the phial of opium into it. Then, with my teeth audibly chattering, I raised the flask to my mouth and pretended to take a long draught, smacking my lips at the end with every appearance of enjoyment.

This, as I thought, proved too much for the Cossacks and their interest was promptly transferred to the flask. I affected to be highly indignant and I went so far as to curse them with every word I could lay my tongue to, and in those days I knew how to swear. The sergeant roared with laughter and with mock ferocity picked up one of my pistols which were on his saddle-bow — for they had disarmed me on my capture — and threatened me with it. My pretended indignation turned thereupon to false fright and I clasped my hands in an exaggerated attitude of supplication. I was the picture of woe, the over-civilised in the grip of the savage-wild. The savage-wild was convinced and satisfied. The pistol was replaced in the holster and the Cossack sergeant raised my flask to his lips. He drank deeply and then reluctantly handed it to his anxious companion. Luckily the flask was large.

The three Cossack troopers drank in turn and the last of them held the flask upside-down with a playful gesture before tossing it into the snow.

All this time, you must understand, we had been jogging slowly on at a walk, and I could tell by the movement of Aigle that he was already somewhat recovered from his fatigue.

Keenly I watched the three men and the sergeant for the next quarter of an hour. Minute after minute passed, and nothing happened.

" *Sacré nom*," I said to myself, " they have heads as hard as a twelve-pound cannon-ball."

Presently, however, to my relief, one of them began

to sing. He was soon joined by the others, but they did not sing for long. Two of them began almost at once to sway in their saddles, while the third collapsed suddenly, shot forward over his horse's shoulder and sprawled in the snow.

At that we all drew rein. The sergeant swore — at least I think he was swearing — and, fumbling vaguely for his lance, prodded solemnly at the prostrate man. At that moment, however, one of his other men, whose swaying had increased, fell against him and collapsed across his horse's neck. Glancing over my shoulder, I saw that the Cossack in the rear was in no better case. He had thrust his lance into the ground and was leaning on it, nodding sleepily, while his horse stood motionless, the breath from its nostrils rising in thin steam on the cold air.

I kicked Aigle in the ribs and, bearing hard on the left rein, swung round abruptly.

" *Au revoir*, Messieurs," I said mockingly with a wave of the hand.

I jerked Aigle into a slow canter, the maximum speed of which he was capable at that moment.

But I had reckoned without the sergeant. With a noise between a shout and a hiccup, he wheeled his horse about, snatching as he did so at my pistols on his saddle. I was thirty yards away by that time, and could only just see him, a dark gesticulating figure against the background of snow. But, even as I looked, there came a blinding flash. He had fired, and that was the last I knew.

§ 7

When I came to myself, I was lying in the snow, stiff as a board. There was a state in my mouth which I will not describe; my tongue felt like the bottom of a parrot's cage, and my head felt oddly tight, as though I was wearing too small a hat. Putting up my hand, I found that I was hatless, but that there was a large lump, covered with matted hair, over my right ear. I began to appreciate what had happened. The bullet from the Cossack's pistol, or rather my pistol, had carried away my shako, and at the same time struck me a glancing blow in the skull, knocking me senseless.

I staggered to my knees, but it must have been ten minutes before I gained sufficient strength to get to my feet. The first thing I saw was Aigle, who stood regarding me with a lack-lustre eye some twenty yards away. Of the Cossacks there was no trace to be seen. Evidently they had ridden away, leaving me there for dead.

It was now almost quite dark. Only the faintest of faint illuminations in the west still continued to burn. I reckoned from the appearance of that sky that I had been unconscious for about half an hour, though I could not tell exactly, for my watch was gone. Anyhow there was still time. That was my first and became my only thought as my scattered wits came slowly together. Gritting my teeth, for my head seemed to be opening and shutting like the lid of a jug, I got into the saddle.

The ride that followed was a nightmare. Luckily, after some time — how long I do not know — I fell in with a troop of chasseurs belonging to Augereau's corps. They guided me to Neidenburg but I scarcely spoke to them. I had only one thought in my head, to reach Marshal Bernadotte. I kept saying to myself over and over again, " Bernadotte . . . Strassburg . . . Bernadotte."

I found myself, at last, clattering up a narrow street deep in mud, with filthy houses on either side shewing up in the glare of bivouac fires. The young Lieutenant at my side pointed to a building, larger than the rest, outside which two sentries were posted. It was lit by a lantern hung above the door.

"There is the Marshal's headquarters, *mon capitaine*," he said.

"Whose?" I asked.

"The quarters of Marshal Augereau," he said. "You are on his staff, are you not? What you want now is a bed and some food, but you'll find it difficult to get either, I'm afraid, in this damned hole."

But I scarcely heard what he said.

"That is no good," I answered. "I want Marshal Bernadotte. I carry dispatches, and must find him tonight."

I do not know what the young officer of chasseurs said, but at that moment we reached the door of headquarters. There were several horses held by a groom standing near to a bivouac fire. I half slipped, half fell from the back of Aigle and staggered towards the groom.

"To whom do these horses belong?" I said slowly.

The man recognised me. It was Hernier, one of the Marshal's own grooms.

"They belong to His Excellency the Duke de Castiglione," he answered.

"Is any of them fresh?" I asked.

"As fresh as can be expected," he answered. "I am taking the stiffness out of them. Monsieur le Duc will be in the saddle in an hour. It is almost dawn."

"A whole night wasted . . . a whole night," I said to myself, "and Marshal Bernadotte is not yet warned."

I laid hold of the bridle of one of the horses.

"I will take this horse," I said. "Tell His Excellency that Captain de Blanchegarde will be unable to report for duty today. He has urgent dispatches from the Marshal Berthier to Marshal Bernadotte. He has taken the liberty in the circumstances of borrowing one of His Excellency's horses."

The groom looked at me with an air of doubt, his hand still on the bridle of a fine light bay, Boule de Cran, which was often ridden by Marshal Augereau himself.

"Quick, man," I said, and thrust my face close into his. It was not a pleasant face. It had two days' growth of beard upon it, there was a smear of blood across the forehead, and the raindrops, for it had turned to rain now, glistened on its moustache and whiskers. The man stepped back and I heaved myself painfully into the saddle.

As I clambered into position, my friend De Viry ran out of the Marshal's headquarters.

"Armand, thank God," he said. "We are glad to have you back, old man."

"I'm not back yet," I gasped. "I must get to Marshal Bernadotte . . . dispatches from the Emperor . . . gone astray."

He must have seen that I was nearly at the end of my tether. He laid a hand on my bridle.

"I will take them," he said. "Hand them over to me and get into my billet here."

But I snatched the bridle from his hand.

"It is no good. Only I can deliver the message. It is here," I said, and I tapped my forehead.

He looked at me strangely.

"No, I am not mad," I said. "The dispatch has been destroyed. It is essential that I should——"

But he did not let me finish.

"Wait two seconds," he said.

He bolted into the doorway, but returned immediately. In his hand was a musty bottle. He thrust it into my trembling grasp.

"Take it, old man," he said. "It may get you to Bernadotte."

It was a bottle of burgundy, and I blessed him.

§ 8

Once more I was on the road. A pale uncertain dawn was coming up over the squalid town. This time my horse was fresh. I learned later that Augereau had decided to ride it himself that day. I got him into a canter, for the road was somewhat better and he swung along at a good pace. My spirits, thanks to the burgundy and the good horse, began to rise. I should yet be in time — that was the thought that fixed itself in my head and the phrase chimed with the rhythm of the horse. I reckoned that the Cossack officer had not had more than an hour's start of me, but he had further to go, and the country through which he had to pass was largely in the hands of our troops. With any luck he might even be captured.

About noon I fell in with a party of hussars, and I recognised them by their facings to be the Ninth. I reined in Boule de Cran and asked the officer in command for news of Marshal Bernadotte's headquarters. They were, it appeared, two leagues further on, in a little village the name of which I forget. This good news put fresh heart into me for I had expected to find him at Strassburg. I shall never forget those last two leagues. The road suddenly became a morass — worse than that, parts of it were flooded, and twice my horse sank over his knees.

At last. . . . There, some two hundred yards ahead of me, was a little church, with a pumpkin spire sticking out above the fir trees. It was two in the afternoon when I saw it and half-past two when I clattered down the village street, paved here and there with rough, uneven stones. I looked for the house of the Marshal and identified it by the sentries posted at the door. I slipped from my horse and pushed my way in without ceremony. No one sought to hinder me. With my bristly face and my streaming hair — for the pistol bullet had knocked my shako off — and my general wild appearance, I was a strange and no doubt a terrifying spectacle.

At the end of the single low-roofed room I found Marshal Bernadotte and three or four of his aides-de-camp. He turned and regarded me, standing tall and lean before the fire. Those eyes of his close together, above the long nose, stared down at me from beneath thick eyebrows. His lips held a smile of welcome, and one hand caressed his mouth and chin, for, as was the fashion among the Marshals of the Empire, he was clean-shaven.

" Your Excellency," I stammered, " I have a message of great importance from the Emperor. The dispatch on which it was written was lost by the officer to whom it was entrusted, but I know its contents."

" Lost," said Bernadotte. " What do you mean ? "

" The officer was captured by Cossacks and killed," I answered. " I also was captured but got away. The dispatch itself is in the hands of the Russians, but it will hardly have got to Bennigsen yet. You still have time to act."

This was to be the great moment of my life. I had arrived in time. The plan of the Emperor was saved. Another brilliant victory, culminating in the complete destruction of an obstinate and dangerous enemy, would be added to the list. And it was I, Armand de Blanche-garde, who had saved the position at the last moment. In spite of my weariness and my aching head I was triumphant and full of joy.

Members of Bernadotte's staff were crowding round me as I spoke, but the Marshal waved them aside. Putting a hand on my shoulder, he drew me towards the fire. We were thus alone, for the rest drew back and stood near the door, waiting the upshot with grave, curious faces.

" What was the dispatch, sir ? " said Bernadotte in a low tone, switching at his boots with the edge of his plumed, cocked hat.

" The Emperor bids you to march on Gilgenburg," I answered, " so that you may join his left. But you are not to march till tonight, sir, and you are to leave behind a body of cavalry to keep up your bivouac fires so that the enemy will think you are still here at Strassburg."

He started at that and then looked at me quizzically.

" Strassburg," he said. " Whence is this message ? "

" I come from Neidenburg, from the headquarters of Marshal Augereau."

" Marshal Augereau is not at Neidenburg," replied Bernadotte. " He left there yesterday."

" Yesterday," I repeated, bewildered.

" He is now moving in the direction of Passenheim, if my latest reports are accurate," continued the Marshal.

" I do not understand," I said feebly. " I started from Neidenburg only five hours ago. Marshal Augereau was still there when I left."

" How do you know that ? " he asked.

" I — er — borrowed the Marshal's horse."

" Then are you sure it was Neidenburg ? " said Bernadotte.

" I never thought to ask, but I concluded that it was. I was there for only a quarter of an hour. They told me at general headquarters yesterday that Marshal Augereau was at Neidenburg and I was proceeding thither to rejoin him when I was captured by the Cossacks."

" When did you leave the Emperor's headquarters ? " asked Bernadotte.

" Yesterday," I replied, " the 31st of January."

He looked at me in amazement.

" Monsieur," he said, " you seem to be under the impression that this is the 1st of February."

I looked at him in utter bewilderment and Bernadotte looked at me — more particularly at the swelling above my right ear.

" Today," he continued, " is not the 1st but the 2nd of February. You say you left the Emperor at Willenburg on the 31st. You have lost a day, Monsieur."

I gazed at him a moment, and then suddenly, overcome, sank upon a stool by the fire and buried my aching head in my hands. I saw at once what had happened. I had been knocked senseless in the snow at sunset. I had come to myself after sunset, but I realised now that it must have been after sunset on the following day. I had lain twenty-four hours unconscious and I had, for all my pains, arrived a day too late to save the Emperor's plan.

I felt a hand on my shoulder. The Marshal was speaking.

" This explains why I have had no orders for thirty-six hours," he said.

I could not raise my head to meet him. My disappointment was too bitter.

" Courage, Monsieur," he added kindly. " You have done all that a man could do."

I raised my head at last and looked at him. He smiled at me courteously.

" Never fear," he said. " We shall catch the Russians yet."

.　　　.　　　.　　　.　　　.　　　.

Yes, my children, we caught them at last ; but it was not until five days later, on the 7th of February, that the battle of Eylau was fought and, as you know, that battle cost us thirty thousand men, and was not a decisive victory. The Emperor has been blamed by the armchair critics for his conduct of that campaign, for very few knew the real reason why things had gone less brilliantly than usual. It was not until the anniversary of Marengo, in the following June, that we finally defeated the Russians at Friedland. Had I not lain twenty-four hours unconscious in the snow it might have been different. That was, perhaps, the most important day in my life — the day I missed between the 31st of January and the 2nd of February 1807.

The Stolen General

SO you thought we looked fine, did you, grouped round the great column with the Emperor — the real Emperor, I mean — on the top of it ? Scarcely one of us could stand to attention, and yet, as you say, *mes enfants*, we were the Grande Armée — twenty-five old fellows from six different regiments, and not one of us will see seventy again. I stood next to Sergeant Keronay, the old man with white hair and the sabre-cut on the left cheek. His bearskin was almost too much for him, though the winter sun was not so very hot. But he fairly sweated. The drops trickled down the ridges in his cheeks till I thought he was crying. Well, perhaps he was. . . . Bearskins of the Old Guard, and a red plume or two of the Polish Lancers, with one brass helmet of the Chasseurs, Jacqueminot or some such name. I never met him. He was junior to me, but he has not lasted as well. He could not wear his helmet, but had to carry it in his hand . . . yes, I know what you're thinking. Lucky for me — isn't it ? that I am a hussar, and didn't have to wear such a heavy uniform ? But you should have seen me getting into my boots this morning, the same I wore at Leipzig, made for me by old Brevier in the rue d'Iéna. It's forty years since I put them on.

You may laugh at an old man, standing with other old men in the sunshine, and watching this new army of yours back from the Crimea — one of the few places we never visited with the Little Corporal. There were one or two who laughed in the crowd today, not many, for it was a fine show and the mob is always ready to do the shouting when others have done the work. The mob shouted all right, but it would shout as loud for a King or a President. This new Emperor hasn't got them to heel like his uncle who looked down at us from his pedestal this afternoon. I remember the day he blew them away from the Tuileries. He knew how to deal with crowds did the little man in the grey coat, with his cold eye and his white kersey breeches, and that twisted gesture of his, the right hand writhing behind his back. Crowds or princes — it was all one to him. I have seen him — stood behind his chair, mind you — when he had eleven kings to dinner.

And it's because of him and of what he did that I stood there this afternoon. I stood there like a fool, Armand de Blanchegarde, General of Division of the Hussars of Angers, and the troops saluted me and the mob roared, and this new Emperor of yours, with his pointed beard and his big moustache and those weak eyes of his, reviewed us.

But he didn't take us by the ear and remind us of the bridge of Lodi and Egypt and Rivoli and the burning houses of Friedland. He had seen no more fighting than a bicker with a douanier or two on the sands of Boulogne, when he set out to capture France in a pleasure steamer. Still he bears the name Napoleon. " *Et 'Poléon, nous l'aurons*," as you have been saying. And about time too. But he is not his uncle, my children, and never will be.

Yes, Gaston, you may pull off my boots. I wore them, as I said, at Leipzig, where they saved my life, but that is another story. Have a care, name of a thousand devils ! Will you take my leg off, too ? These are legs, I tell you, not boot trees.

What is that you say ? Tired ? . . . well . . . it has

*been a longer day than usual and eighty years is eighty
years. Though I am not done yet, my lad, and, maybe,
you will still wait some time before you hear the roll of the
muffled drums.*

Drums . . . I heard them first beside the Pyramids
as we formed square to receive the Mameluks. I was
only nineteen then. And I heard them last at half-past
six on the 18th June, 1815, in front of the Château of
Hougoumont, still held by the English Guards.

*Yes, I know it is past bedtime, Suzanne, but your
mother will let you stay up half an hour. You can eat
your supper here on my knee. But easy now, if you please.
I am not a pack-horse, little hussy.*

What do you want me to tell you ? A story of
Napoleon, the real Napoleon — not the one we saw
today with his cigarettes and his watery blue eye, who
was so patronising to us all ? Very well. Gaston, too,
for all his eighteen years, would like perhaps to hear
another of his grandfather's tales. And true, mind you.
We of the Grande Armée lived history. We have no
need to write it. Come, Gaston . . . more coal on the
fire, and then we will begin. I feel in my old bones that
there is a storm coming up. But what's a storm in
Paris ? I have known storms in my life, and the worst
I was ever in was when I crossed the Danube in a small
boat with five shivering Germans calling on God and
their mothers, and I don't know what, with two of my
grenadiers prodding them now and again just to make
'em feel happier. That was a night, and that, if you like,
shall be the story.

§ 2

You remember the campaign of 1809 ? It's all in
the history books, for those that can read them. It was

a few days after the battle of Eckmühl, the 7th of May, to be exact. I was on the staff of Lannes in those days and not too flourishing, I don't mind telling you. Not that I had anything against Lannes, the finest leader of infantry in the Grande Armée, and good to me, too. He was killed a month later at Aspern, as you all know.

I was only Captain de Blanchegarde then, and had been captain for a year.— ever since Burgos, in fact. They had promised me my step after the siege of Saragossa, but I never got it. The Emperor was busy in those days. He used to sign all the *brevets* himself, and who can blame him if he sometimes fell behind ? Anyhow, there I was, still a captain, and a captain without a sou. I had had two horses killed at Eckmühl, and had just spent my last five louis buying new ones. You could always get your pick after a battle, especially when the Austrians had made one of their futile charges.

Lannes was in command of the advance-guard, and the Emperor was with him. Our cavalry pickets were out beyond Mölk, and my old regiment, the Hussars of Angers, and another unit whose name I forget, were picketed just in front of the village. It had poured with rain all day, and I had spent my time trying to get reports from our cavalry as to the whereabouts of the Austrians. But there was not a word to be had. The Emperor was pretty short-tempered, and, as for Lannes, he was in a raging fury. We had beaten the Austrians at Eckmühl, and now we were marching on Vienna. But the Archduke had the legs of us. The Austrians were the finest troops in retreat I have ever seen. They moved faster than a light-cavalryman after a wench, and we didn't know where on earth they had got to. The Emperor, Lannes told me that afternoon as I had come back for the tenth time with no news, thought they must be retreating to cover Vienna, but he was not sure and it worried him, for he could not pierce their light-cavalry screen. There was not a prisoner to be had. He had offered five hundred francs to anyone who would bring one in to him.

We got fairly comfortably settled in Mölk for the night. The Emperor and Lannes were at the big monastery, staying with the Abbot, or whatever he called himself. A fine place it was, overlooking the river, a huge building with walls thirty feet thick and cellars — *mon dieu*, but they were cellars indeed! And the grenadiers of the Guard may be trusted on a point of that kind.

We of Lannes' staff, except for the aide-de-camp on duty, were billeted on the village priest, not a bad old boy, with some very drinkable burgundy and a pretty niece — at least, he said she was his niece — who kept house for him. We hadn't had anything to eat all day, so when he produced a couple of geese we all voted him a good fellow and allowed him a glass or two of his own wine.

The geese were beginning to look precious small when who should come in but de Bourdigny, who clapped me on the shoulder. De Bourdigny was the aide-de-camp on duty.

" The Marshal wants you at once," he said, as the door slammed behind him.

He was always a noisy fellow, de Bourdigny, till he lost his head at Borodino.

" Out you go, my stout young friend," said Ruec. " Perhaps you will come back a general."

The others laughed at that, for they knew I was pretty sore at not getting my step. Ruec was an old man with grey moustaches. How he got on Lannes' staff I never could imagine. He knew a lot about commissariat and how much weight you could put on a mule, and that sort of thing, but he had the worst seat on a horse of any man I ever saw.

I got to my feet, hitched my sword up, slung my sodden dolman over my shoulder and, clapping on my shako, followed de Bourdigny down the village. It was raining as though heaven had sprung a leak, and there was the devil of a wind that howled down the narrow street and all the way along the winding alley we followed to get to the monastery.

"What in the name of the devil can Lannes want with me tonight?" I asked de Bourdigny as we swung along.

"I don't know," he said. "He was with the Emperor half an hour ago. They were standing on the balcony which overlooks the river. Then he came out and sent me straight for you."

I shook the water from my shako and strode on. Had my *brevet* come at last? I had seen Berthier's secretary only the day before with a whole armful of *portefeuilles*. Perhaps the Emperor had signed a few. But why should the Marshal drag me from a comfortable dinner to give me my *brevet* when he could just as easily have given it to me the next morning?

Ten o'clock sounded from the church as we swung left and found ourselves opposite the gate of the monastery. There was a guard there, grenadiers of the Old Guard, in their big bearskins. The men not on duty were round a fire in the courtyard, for there was no shelter and they were doing what they could to keep dry. . . .

What's that, Suzanne? . . . Yes, of course, they all

74

wore moustaches. Like mine. Not so fine or long perhaps, but still moustaches. You had to wear a moustache in the Guard, and if you could not grow one you made one out of wax. Those were the orders. . . .

We passed the fire and entered the monastery itself. The lower hall was empty except for a couple of the Emperor's lackeys, who bowed and sent us to the major-domo, who took us up a broad oak stairway till we reached a long corridor. That was like the Emperor. He kept his state in full campaign. That was to impress the fools. He knew a thing or two, did the Emperor. Come to think of it, he impressed us all with it, more or less.

Opening upon the long corridor were a number of large *salons*, guest chambers, I suppose, for the monastery was very rich, one of the richest in Austria ; and it entertained on a lavish scale. The corridor was full, but not as full as the *salons*. De Bourdigny took me into one on the left — packed with generals, aides-de-camp and several officers of the Emperor's personal staff. Among them were St. Hilaire, Pouzet and Carra St. Cyr. They were standing a little apart from the rest in an embrasure formed by the window, and they looked up curiously as I came in by the door.

De Bourdigny pushed his way forward with me at his heels to where a door opened into what I supposed was another *salon*. Before we reached it, however, it was flung violently open, and a man of middle height, in a magnificent coat of blue and gold and a white satin waistcoat, stood in the doorway.

" Where's this Captain de Blanchegarde ? " he said.

It was General Bertrand, and my heart missed a beat. Was I going to get my *brevet* after all ? I moved forward, but stepped to the left, for St. Hilaire was advancing to speak to General Bertrand. Bertrand, however, waved him aside.

"One moment, General," he said. "The Emperor is asking for Captain de Blanchegarde."

"I am here, *mon général*," I replied.

"You are to come with me," he said quickly.

He signed to de Bourdigny to remain where he was, shook his head at a whispered question from St. Hilaire, and, turning on his heel, beckoned me to follow.

§ 3

I found myself in an immense room. Not as big, Suzanne, as the Galerie des Glaces at Versailles, but very nearly. It must have stretched the whole length of one side of the monastery, more of a gallery than a room, for the whole of one side was a series of windows, like great arches, half of them unglazed, with balconies overlooking the Danube. The room was brilliantly lit, with clusters of wax candles which flickered and smoked a good deal, for there was a heavy draught. Beyond the light I got a glimpse of swirling water and trees bent with the wind. But I had no eyes for such things. The Emperor was asking to see *me*, Armand de Blanchegarde. I followed General Bertrand across the long stone floor to an alcove at the further end of the room, in which was set a table covered with a white cloth. The blood was singing in my ears.

The Emperor was at dinner, seated beside the Abbot of the monastery, who was at his right hand. Several Marshals were with him, among them Lannes, Bernadotte and Masséna. They were laughing, and loudest of them all was the Abbot, a jovial, fat fellow, dressed in the black of his Order — he was a Benedictine — with a great cross on his breast. There were one or two bottles on the table and a large dish of fruit in front of the Emperor, piled so high that for the moment I did not see him very well.

As we moved rapidly across the floor, however, he caught sight of Bertrand. He rose instantly and beckoned to Lannes. The table was now very silent. Lannes had risen too, and Napoleon, taking him by the arm, moved away from the table to my right and out through one of the windows on to the balcony. His face was white in the candle-light. I stood stiffly beside the table, looking only towards the Emperor out on the balcony. He began to speak rapidly to Lannes in a low tone. There were lines of doubt about his mouth. Lannes was not much taller than he, and did not need to bend his head to hear what the Emperor was saying.

I found myself suddenly alone. Bertrand was sitting now at the table and had poured himself out a glass of burgundy. Clicking my heels together, so that the spurs jingled, I drew myself up to attention and waited. I could think of nothing for the moment, except that there before me was the Emperor. I had seen him a score of times. Had I not served on his staff at Marengo when he was First Consul ? And yet, when he turned his head abruptly and looked me up and down, the old thrill ran through me again. That is a thrill you will never feel under your new Emperor, not if he wins a hundred battles — no, not if he fulfils his uncle's dream and you help to batter down the gates of Delhi.

" Is this the man ? "

It was the Emperor speaking. His voice was dry and cold. For there was I, a soldier, on parade.

" Yes, Sire," answered Lannes.

" You answer for him ? "

" You need a man. He is the best of them all."

You understand, my children, I am only telling you what he said. I make no comment. He said I was the best of them all. Lannes was a magnificent soldier.

The Emperor looked at me very straight for a moment or so.

" Do you know anything of strategy, Captain de Blanchegarde ? " he said at last.

" A little, Sire."

" Come over here," said the Emperor, and I moved forward two paces till I was directly opposite him. He took me by the arm, drawing me aside, so that we stood together facing the night. The wind howled about us, and an occasional gust of rain beat on the balcony. The Emperor stretched out his hand.

" What do you see ? " he asked.

At our feet was a tossing mass of black water — the Danube in spate, dark and murky, to be distinguished rather by the ear than by the eye except where an occasional light from some unshuttered casement in the village below flickered suddenly upon the driven waves.

" That is the Danube, Sire," I stammered.

" And the lights yonder, on the further side. Whose are they ? "

" The Austrians, Sire."

" Whose corps ? "

" That, Sire, is too hard a question."

Napoleon looked at me.

" Whom do you think we were pursuing today, Captain de Blanchegarde ? "

" The Archduke Charles, perhaps."

That, my children, was a foolish answer, but I was expected to say something. " Perhaps " is no word for a soldier.

" Captain de Blanchegarde," said the Emperor, " I will give you a lesson in strategy. We are on the right bank of the Danube. The Archduke Charles is certainly on the left. But the Austrians have a rear-guard."

" Naturally, Sire," I ventured. " The enemies of France have often found it necessary."

The Emperor smiled, but only for a moment.

" Where is the Austrian rear-guard ? " he continued. " That is what I must know, and I must know at once and for certain. General Hiller is in command. Has he crossed the Danube, and is he now over there with the Archduke Charles, or has the Archduke left him to oppose me here tomorrow at St. Polten ? If General Hiller has passed the Danube, the way is open and I shall be in Vienna in two days. Where is General Hiller ? Can you find that out for me, Captain de Blanchegarde ? "

He looked at me keenly as he spoke, and I looked back at the Emperor, which was a little difficult, for he was, as you know, a short man and I stood six feet four in those days, before this cursed rheumatism bent my back. Then I looked over his head at the black river Danube, and the long line of flickering lights on the far side that marked the Austrian bivouacs. I saw what was in his mind, and I did not speak for a moment. My mouth had suddenly gone dry. For there was only one way of finding out whether General Hiller and his corps had crossed the river.

" You understand what His Majesty means, de Blanchegarde ? " Lannes was saying. " If General Hiller has joined the Archduke on the other side of the river, there is nothing now between us and Vienna but a thin screen of cavalry. If General Hiller has not yet

G

crossed, it means a big engagement tomorrow."

" I understand, Your Excellency," said I.

I was looking at the lights of the Austrian bivouacs, and at that instant a great gust of wind and rain burst upon us, rattling against the glass and shaking the half-open window which Lannes was holding so that the Emperor could look through and not be bothered with the reflection on the pane.

" It is not an order that I give you, Captain de Blanchegarde," said the Emperor, breaking our silence abruptly. " It is a mission I ask you to undertake. I am well aware of its difficulties. If you refuse I shall not think the worse of you. Go into the anteroom and come back in five minutes with your decision."

I clicked my heels and made to withdraw as he bade me. But I had scarcely taken half a dozen steps when I turned back again. My mind was on fire. The Emperor had twenty-five thousand of his Guard in, and around, the monastery of Mölk. The ante-rooms were packed with his Generals and his aides. And yet, when it came to a mission that required courage and intelligence, he had sent for me, your old grandfather, who was nearly run down yesterday by one of these new-fangled omnibuses of yours.

I returned to the Emperor.

" I am ready, Sire," I said. " You shall have my report before dawn."

He nodded abruptly, and gave me that shining look of his which had sent many a proud man to his death before me. Then he went back to the table to where the Abbot was cracking nuts and jokes with Masséna and Bernadotte.

" Your Lordship is doubtless right," I heard the second remark, as I stood gazing after the Emperor.

" Clothes were invented by woman in order to invite, and not to defeat, our curiosity."

There was a laugh from the table and a jingling of spurs and clanking of scabbards as the Emperor joined them and picked up his coffee-cup.

But Lannes was breathing heavily in my ear.

" There is Bertrand," he said. " He will give you your orders. I knew you would not fail me, and I am sure you will not fail the Emperor."

" I am most grateful to Your Excellency," I began.

" *Chut*, man ! " he said, cutting me short, " we will talk about that tomorrow."

" *M. le maréchal*," I was thinking, " you are an optimist."

Bertrand joined us as we moved down the long gallery towards another door that I had not noticed.

" It is decided then," he said. " I have already made the arrangements."

" A boat seems indicated, *mon général*," I answered. " It is a cold night for a swim, and I was not born with wings."

He smiled at that and signed to a servant, who threw open the door. A sound of crying interspersed with oaths and protestations in a foreign tongue met our ears.

§ 4

We passed into a small room hung with faded tapestry. The uncouth sounds proceeded from four or five men who were grouped in front of the broad hearth, in which a fire of logs was burning. They were dressed in rough homespun and had great boots on their feet with which, when they moved, they made a most infernal clatter on the stone floor.

I glanced at General Bertrand with raised eyebrows.

"Those are your guides," he said. "The five best watermen in Mölk, so the syndic assures me."

He clapped heartily upon the shoulder a fat little man in a shiny brown suit with enormous brass buttons to his long waistcoat, who came forward bowing until I thought his forehead would knock against his knees.

"That is so, Your Excellency," said the syndic, speaking in execrable French. "The five best watermen in Mölk, as Your Excellency says. There is none better than Johan, Fritz and Zwangli here. But what would Your Excellency? They say it is death to cross the river tonight. Being such excellent watermen, they ought to know. I have myself lived fifty years in Mölk, and you can tell the Emperor from me, with my deepest respect——"

Bertrand cut him short with a gesture.

"I know what you would say," he said abruptly, "and it is not to the purpose. Tell these men, *M. le Syndic*, to commend their souls to God and their bodies to my friend here, Captain de Blanchegarde. They will either go or hang."

Bertrand was a man of few words, like most of the Emperor's staff. Their master set the measure and they followed it.

"Captain de Blanchegarde," he went on, "do you speak German?"

"Not a word, sir," said I.

"Well," said he, "it is not of much consequence. The corporal in charge of the escort speaks it well. So do they all, in fact. They are from Alsace."

There was a sound of trampling feet as he spoke, and a door on the further side of the room opened to admit a corporal and two files of the grenadiers of the Guard.

This was to be my escort, and my heart rose at the sight of them. They filed into the room, with a mechanical clatter and precision which is music to the ears of a soldier.

" *A droite. Marquez le pas. Peloton — halte.*"

The corporal, an elderly man with a grey moustache, came forward and saluted.

" *Peloton*, for special duty, present and correct, sir."

" Here are your men, Captain," said General Bertrand, turning as he spoke. " The rest is for you, and you have *carte blanche*. Good luck to you."

He moved across the room as he spoke, and had now reached the door by which we had entered. I stood silent a moment. Behind me twittered the five miserable watermen, great louts, undisciplined and afraid. In front of me were the five stalwart grenadiers of the Guard, their bearskins nodding above their heavy moustaches, their eyes looking straight to the front, their backs as stiff as ramrods.

" Good luck," said General Bertrand again as he pushed open the door, and then he added softly :

" *Vive l'Empereur.*"

The words crashed out behind me as I turned to salute him. The five grenadiers spoke in unison, and the shout that had been heard on twenty battlefields smote the little room, so that the quaking watermen were still, and eyed the five men and their leader in fearful admiration.

I turned to my new command.

" Stand at ease," I said, and then, immediately, " As you were."

" Smarter than that, lads," I bade them. " You are of the Guard, remember."

The corporal eyed me oddly, but I knew my job.

Make a man drill smartly, and he will do anything, go through the deadliest breach as if it were a paper hoop. I stood them at ease again and turned to the corporal.

"Your name," I asked.

"Corporal Cobeaux," he answered. "Eight years' service, undecorated."

"You speak German, Corporal," said I.

"Yes, *mon capitaine*, we are all of us from Alsace."

"Then tell those quaking fellows to be ready," I said, pointing to the watermen.

The corporal went over to the men by the hearth and spoke to them in their strange tongue. The German language is not elegant, and, as spoken by the corporal, seemed as nasty to the five poor wretches who spoke it as it did to me. Two of them fell on their knees. The other three huddled back over the fire.

"They say it is certain death, *mon capitaine*," replied the Corporal.

"Tell them," I answered, "that if it is certain death to go, it is equally certain death to stay. Hanging or drowning, my friends — and let them choose quickly."

The corporal addressed them again, while I moved forward and stood beside him, drawing myself up to my full height, and letting the end of my scabbard fall with a clash on the stone floor. One of the five watermen, who seemed to be braver than the rest, a man in the fifties with a bushy black beard — Fritz was his name — shambled forward and raised his hand to his forehead in a rough gesture of respect. He said something which Corporal Cobeaux translated.

"He repeats that it is certain death," said the corporal, "but that they will do their best."

"Stout fellows," I answered. "March them down to the wharf and be ready to start in twenty minutes."

The corporal marshalled his men, who formed up behind the fishermen, and in a few moments the room was empty. I followed more at my leisure, and I must confess that in the street I began to be sorry for the fishermen. The Danube was in spate and nearly twice as broad at that point as it should be. There was a fierce storm and the night was darker than usual owing to the rain. " Certain death," they had said, and they probably knew what they were talking about. From their point of view things could hardly have been worse. For me, as a landsman and a soldier, the foul weather would have its compensations, once we got across the river. You will find few sentries alert on a dark night in a torrent of rain.

My problem, of course, was to get into touch with the Austrian sentries. The watch-fires which I had seen from the balcony in the company of the Emperor were directly opposite us on the other side of the river. We should have, therefore, to move a considerable distance up-stream before we attempted to cross ; for if we did not do so, the current, being very strong, would sweep us far down-stream and we might lose the Austrian Army altogether.

Beside the jetty, which in normal times was high and dry, but which on that night was covered by a torrent of water, I found my five fishermen, surrounded by a noisy crowd, preparing a fairly large and seemingly watertight craft. It had a short mast set well forward and a single large sail. In addition there were four pairs of oars. The old corporal was urging them on with the work, paying no attention to the crowd, most of whom were women. They set up a veritable howl on my approach, whether of rage or entreaty I could not say. I did not know German, and for the moment I was glad. After all, they were women, and one of them — the one who made the most noise — was pretty. I do not like to argue with women.

"Send a man to collect your forage caps," I said, as the corporal saluted. "You can't cross the Danube in bearskins. Tell him also to call at my billet on the way back and bring me my *képi*."

The corporal shouted the order, and one of the grenadiers moved off at the double. I watched carefully the furnishing of the boat. She was, as I have said, stout and well built. There was a somewhat clumsy rudder in the stern and a rusty anchor hanging by a chain in the bows. Remembering a trick I had seen used by fishermen on the Rhône near Arles, I ordered the anchor to be removed, and substituted for it two canvas sacks secured to the boat by two lengths of rope. The sacks I had filled with two or three large round stones. By the time these preparations were complete, my grenadier had returned with the forage caps and my *képi*.

With him came the village priest.

"I beseech you, sir," he said to me in French, "grant me a moment to pray with these poor men who are risking their lives for your sake." At the sight of the priest one of the fishermen abandoned the boat and fell on his knees.

"*Gott . . . Gott . . . Gott . . .*" he said three or four times.

"Comfort him, father," said I. "Tell him I trust that there is no need for him yet to think of God. And time is short."

"One moment, Excellency," said the priest, "my duty forbids that any man should go to his death unprepared."

"Pray then for me as well," said I, "but be brief and to the point."

86

Yes, my children. I was ever a religious man, and a prayer in need is a prayer indeed. But I am not one to worry heaven with trifles. Do what you can for yourself, and God may do the rest.

The priest prayed with them a moment and blessed them. I bowed with reverence, and his raised hand, very beautiful with long tapering fingers, moved with a spacious gesture above our heads. On lifting my eyes, I perceived that his other hand was also beautiful, for it held two bottles of burgundy, and he thrust them in my direction as he finished the benediction. In a trice the necks were off, and each man had a glass of wine, in the glow of which we all jumped into the boat.

§ 5

A moment later we were afloat on the Danube. I was in the stern, and Fritz was at the tiller. I was glad to note that the fishermen, now that they were aboard, were resolved to make the best of it. Each man to his own particular courage. Mine is for the land, and I don't mind confessing that, during the next half-hour, I suffered several sorts of death on that confounded river. At the start, in accordance with the plan I had hastily thought out on my way down to the jetty, we kept close in to the shore and sailed, not across but steadily up-stream. Fortunately, the wind, though violent, favoured this manœuvre, and we proceeded in this manner for the best part of a league, keeping as far as we could to the lee of the bank, which was very high. The spirits of my grenadiers began to rise.

" Name of a name," said one of them, " this is better than those cursed English seas at Boulogne. We sail here for our pleasure."

I did not undeceive him. All in good time he would learn what was in store.

I leaned over to Corporal Cobeaux.

"Corporal," I said, "I think we are far enough up-river by now. Bid them put forth into the stream."

He spoke to Fritz, who, setting his teeth, swung the tiller over. The boat's nose moved round to the left, and the clumsy sail shot out at right angles to our craft. The boat reeled. Hans, after one look at the taut canvas, leaped forward. He thrust an axe at one of his men and shouted an order. It was easy enough to see what we were to do for safety. To shorten sail in such a gale was hopeless, and the fellow, taking the axe, began frantically to cut the sail free. It was a near thing, and the mast crashed over just as the dark water began to pour over the gunwale.

Even then we nearly upset. Yes, my children, being in a boat is not like being in a stage-coach. A boat is subject to the wind and, if too much water enters, you sink. I explain all this that you may understand. The more civilised races are not made for boats. For them is the land. The perfidious English hold the sea, and to fight them there was always, in my view, a mistake. Their Nelson, they say, was a wonderful fighter. But then, he never met the Emperor. I would like to have seen him and his English sailors at Austerlitz or Friedland.

Well, we got rid of the mast and sail and felt all the easier in consequence. Your English tricksters might have used them, but we had more sense than to gamble with the wind. Four pairs of oars were good enough for us, and our fishermen bent their backs to them finely.

We had made a dozen yards or so when a long dark object swept suddenly past us, and before I had recovered from the fright it gave me, there was a shock as though somebody had driven a battering-ram into the side of the boat. I did not ask what it was, remembering what I had seen that evening. There were a lot of logs in the Danube that year; they had been cut in the spring and had floated down, and they were all over the river. Some of them were great pine-trunks, big enough to stave in the side of a house. One of the fishermen began to curse or to pray — I do not know which — and God Himself in that language of theirs must find it difficult to distinguish — and Fritz looked at me with a question in his eyes, hoping that even I might be wishing to turn back. But were the plans of the Emperor to be ruined by a log of wood? We would go on if we were to face a whole forest of floating timber. Fortunately the log had struck us only a glancing blow, and we had not sprung a leak.

I remembered the way in which they used to row the Roman galleys in classical times. Not that I ever paid much attention to the classics when I was at Sorèze under the good Bernard Ferlas, but there are some things that stick in the memory, and I recalled how they had a master oarsman — a sort of sergeant-major of rowers, who gave them the time and kept them in step so that the galley moved forward like a column of the Old Guard. Discipline, said I to myself, that is the secret of success; and, if discipline is necessary on land, how much more is it necessary on the unstable water!

I pulled out my pistol, whereupon one of the crew, mistaking my intentions, dropped his oar and, so far as I could gather, begged me not to blow out his brains. I regretted profoundly this misunderstanding, for I was beginning to like my German ruffians.

I explained my intention to Corporal Cobeaux.

" Tell these fellows," said I, " to take their time from me and row by the right."

I took the pistol by the barrel and beat the side of the boat in a regular rhythm so that the rowers could keep together. After that we got on better, though if I beat too fast the bow oarsman lost his alignment. But my friends who row tell me that the bow oarsman is always late.

So we went on across the Danube, making a good deal of leeway, you understand, but none the less slowly approaching the Austrian camp-fires. I was in mortal terror lest the current should be too strong and sweep us past the Austrian camp altogether, in which case we should fail of our purpose, for we had no chance, now mast and sail were gone, to beat our way back against the current. Fate, however, was kind, for we presently came under the lee of what seemed to be a floating forest, though one of the fishermen said it was an island completely submerged by the flood. Twice we were entangled in the trees, and had to cut our way through with axes.

When we at last got clear we found ourselves in calmer water, and now we were not more than a hundred yards from the shore. Here again the luck was with us. For the bank of the Danube was in that place covered with a long straggling line of willow trees, thick and bushy with early summer foliage leaning well over the water. This made it difficult for anyone to approach the bank, but made it equally difficult for the Austrians to see us, which was as well, for, though the wind was as fierce as ever, the rain had stopped, while a slim moon was playing hide-and-seek among the clouds. The watch-fires of the Austrians were not more than fifty yards from the bank.

It was here that my canvas sacks full of stones came in useful. I ordered the fishermen to rest on their oars, while Corporal Cobeaux, who had received his instructions before we started, moved into the bows of the boat, holding one of the sacks to which was attached a stout length of cord. As soon as we stopped rowing the boat began to drift, and began slowly to approach the willows. I went forward and joined the corporal, looking for some place where a landing might be practicable. I soon saw one about twenty yards ahead of us, an open space, muddy and trampled, where the Austrians had taken their horses down to water. I nudged the corporal, for no word must now be spoken, and he flung the bag of stones with great effect into the branches of the nearest willow. It wrapped itself two or three times round the branches just as I had seen ropes similarly flung cling hold of the willow trees bordering the Rhône. Our boat pulled up with a jerk.

We were now securely anchored, and the first part of my mission was successfully accomplished. The willow to which we were attached was not two yards from the watering-place used by the Austrians. For a moment we lay silent, rocking gently. No sound came from the Austrian camp. It must have been near midnight. The Austrians, separated from the Grande Armée by the whole width of the Danube, did not trouble to keep a close watch, and from where I crouched, I could see only two sentries moving up and down. I perceived that we had come to the bank opposite an Austrian battery of twelve-pounders, trained to fire on the village of Mölk across the river.

The hardest part of my task had now to be accomplished. I was somehow to secure a prisoner without waking the sleeping host, and thus finding myself in a hornets' nest. I took whispered counsel with the corporal. Obviously our best hope was to surprise the two sentries whom we could see pacing up and down not fifty yards away, but to capture a man on sentry-go, and carry him off without making a sound, is no easy matter, as you may well imagine. I turned round and whispered to the five fishermen, telling them to lie flat in the bottom of the boat. I then told two of my grenadiers to keep a strict eye on them, and to run a bayonet through any one of them who attempted to move or utter a sound. Then, followed by the corporal and the other two grenadiers, I stepped ashore, scrambling with some little difficulty through the branches of the willow tree.

We crept forward slowly, keeping well in the shelter of the willow trees, and I still wondered how I should attack the sentry. The confounded fellow was wide awake — evidently not a conscript, but a seasoned soldier who knew his job.

Something damp was thrust into my hand. It was a neck-cloth full of wet sand.

" Clap it over his face, sir," whispered the corporal. " One of us will catch his musket and the other will take him round the knees."

I nodded. This corporal certainly had a head on his shoulders.

We had now, you understand, reached the last of the willows, and there was nothing between us and the unconscious sentry. There was not a scrap of cover, and still more than twenty yards to cross. We should have to wait until his back was turned, and make a dash for it.

I was explaining all this to the corporal in whispers, when suddenly there came a man's voice singing softly in the night. He was humming an air from some

Austrian love-song. I nudged my corporal, who nudged his men, and we all lay close. Here, indeed, was a piece of good fortune. We could see the singer now. He was moving carelessly down the clearing towards the water, swinging a small bucket, and as he went, we kept pace with him in the shadows. At the edge of the water he paused, looked for a moment over the river, and then bent down to fill his bucket. In an instant I jumped up, thrust my foot firmly into his backside, while the corporal and one of my grenadiers seized him by the nape of his neck and pushed his head into his own bucket or into the Danube, I am not quite sure which. In a trice the fellow was trussed up, gagged with a wet handkerchief and thrust into the boat before he knew what had happened to him.

So far so good. But, on taking a look at our prisoner I was not entirely satisfied. The man we had caught was not, strictly speaking, a combatant, but some sort of officer's servant, and as such, he might not be able to supply the information desired by the Emperor. The Austrian officers, you understand, especially the higher born, took their own valets with them when on a campaign. I debated what to do. Should I be content with the fish we had caught, or tempt Fortune further, and have a shot at the sentry?

I was not required, however, to make up my mind, for, even as I turned, there was a heavy clatter of arms on the bank above us, and, looking up, I saw the sentry we had thought to attack standing stiffly to attention at the present. A little man, dressed in a white uniform, obviously the picket officer going his rounds, was passing him. I could see them both outlined against the bivouac fires. I noticed another thing. The sentry was at the present. The man in the white uniform was, therefore, a field officer, perhaps the *Chef de Brigade*, making the round himself. Here was a bit of luck, for he would know all about General Hiller and the whereabouts of his corps.

At the mere sight of him I lost all sense of caution. A sixth sense, intuition, or whatever you may call it, told me that this was the supreme moment of my career. Down beside the river was Captain de Blanchegarde and three grenadiers of the Old Guard. But the Austrian Army was asleep, and Captain de Blanchegarde and his grenadiers were awake.

" Stand up, men," I whispered. " Obey my orders and it is the Cross for us all."

The men got to their feet, and at that moment the moon swam clear, its beams flashing on my sabre. I drew myself up to my full height and stepped into the moonlight.

" Grenadiers of the Guard," I shouted in my parade voice, " *En avant — au pas de charge*," and with a shout of " *Vive l'Empereur !* " we made straight for the astonished Austrian officer and the motionless sentry.

We had scarcely twenty yards of open ground to cover, and I made for the Austrian officer. He was a little man, and I could not see him very clearly, for the moon had dodged behind a cloud again. I noted, however, that he was in some kind of mess uniform, white with blue and gold braid and gold epaulets. There was a star on his breast.

" Surrender, or you are a dead man," I said, and ferociously I grabbed at the collar of his tunic. At the same moment there were three or four crisp detonations behind me. My grenadiers had fired a volley before the charge. The sentry, who was still standing at attention, his musket at the present, swayed and toppled, and I saw a dark stain appear as though by magic on his face. His musket fell with a clatter, and he pitched forward to the ground. A tall, lean man in a dark uniform appeared like a genius behind the little officer in white, while shouts and clashes a little way off shewed me that my grenadiers were also heavily engaged.

My sabre struck a shower of sparks from that of the tall, lean man, but it was all over in a second. I disengaged in tierce, made a swift riposte over his wrist, and my point entered his throat two inches below the chin. He staggered and fell and at the same instant I saw old Corporal Cobcaux at my side, his bayonet dripping. All this time, you understand, I had hold of the little Austrian officer by the scruff of his neck. I had met easily enough his tall, thin friend with my right.

The whole thing can scarcely have lasted a full minute, and the little Austrian officer was still tugging at his sword when I ran his companion through. I brought my hilt sharply down on the back of his neck. He gave a hiccup and then grew limp in my grasp. I bent down, dropping my sabre as I did so, and threw him over my shoulder like a sack. Then I turned back and doubled for the boat, shouting to my men to retreat. Corporal Cobeaux took in the situation at a glance. He bellowed a series of commands, as though he had a whole regiment of the Guard instead of two men, one of whom, though I only learned it afterwards, was already dead, and we retreated smartly towards the bank. There we met my other two grenadiers, for at the sound of the shots they had scrambled ashore and had come to join in the fray.

"Back to the boat," I shouted, and in another moment I had reached it myself and pitched into it the inanimate Austrian officer.

There was no time for stepping delicately, but it took us some moments to get aboard. It is no easy matter, let me tell you, to climb into a plunging boat when you are wearing riding-breeches, and, as I scrambled and swore, I had a vivid impression of what was happening in the hornets' nest we had so successfully awakened. Pandemonium was by this time raging in the Austrian line. There were shouts and cries and, what was worse, the unmistakeable booming of a non-commissioned officer, doubtless ordering the gunners to stand to their pieces. At any other time I might have been flattered by such attention. It is not every day that a French officer and five men has the honour to find himself the target for a whole battery of guns ; but, when you are less than fifty yards off, struggling to get into a boat and cut it free, it is not so amusing. And yet, my children, will you believe me when I say that even in that moment I could not help thinking what a glorious death it would be ? The guns would sound and their thunder would be heard by the Emperor on his balcony, searching the darkness with his keen eyes, and he would know that Armand de Blanchegarde had died as a soldier of France. That would be glory indeed, and no one would ever know that at its supreme moment I was hanging head-first over the edge of a rocking boat, waving my big boots in the air and presenting to the Austrian Army a target such as a gentleman seldom presents to the enemy.

But those guns were never fired. For, as one of my grenadiers yanked me into the boat, and I caught sight of the Austrian gunners whirling their lighted matches round their heads, three or four officers came running up, and I heard the stentorian voice of the master gunner shouting an order. Whereupon his men, instead of touching off the guns, stood easy with their matches and nothing further happened. I could not think what on earth had taken them. Neither for the moment did I care, but began to hack fiercely with an axe at the rope which bound us to the willow tree. The rope was stubborn, and at every blow the boat jumped like a bucking horse. At last, however, it parted with a snap, and in an instant we were adrift and spinning away into the Danube. But the fishermen had their oars out in a trice and, realising that their lives depended on it, set to work and rowed for dear life. Soon we were back again in mid-stream, and there remained little for me to do, being a landsman, but to hope for the best.

The little officer in the white uniform woke up when we were about half-way across, and when he realised what was happening was most profane. He grew positively purple, in fact, and swore in the oddest mixture of French and German, so that it was a pleasure to hear him. His eloquence became somewhat tedious after a while, and at last Corporal Cobeaux could stand it no longer and started groping at the bottom of the boat. He soon found what he wanted, and, turning round, clapped over the head of our prisoner the second of the canvas bags which we had taken in reserve and from which he had emptied the stones.

The journey back was uneventful except that, once or twice, we were bumped by the swimming logs, and we finally came to land a good deal below Mölk.

At one time I feared that the stream would carry us too far down, and that we should miss the outposts altogether, but very fortunately we struck the bank opposite a picket of the Ninth Hussars commanded by Colonel Gautrin, if I remember rightly. They were part of Lannes' Corps, and they had with them an aide-de-camp, Viry or some such name, who knew all about

97

my mission. I need not tell you that no time was lost. In less than five minutes he had me and my little Austrian astride two horses belonging to the picket, and galloping for Mölk. My prisoner was swearing no longer, though, of course, the canvas bag had by that time been removed. He had passed the limits of speech. All he could do was to swallow his wrath, and there were moments when I thought it would choke him.

We clattered into the courtyard of the monastery as dawn was breaking, and were taken without a moment's delay up the staircase and along the corridor. There was no waiting in the anteroom, and we passed quickly between lines of smiling faces. Old General St. Hilaire, I remember, clapped me on the shoulder as I passed.

But I had no time to give to my friends. I had still to make my report to the Emperor.

There at last he was, with Lannes beside him. Neither of them appeared to have gone to bed that night.

Napoleon strode forward, a hand thrust into his waistcoat. You know the gesture. It is famous. I halted at the regulation distance, and clapped my heels so that the spurs jingled.

" Captain de Blanchegarde, Sire. I have the honour to present prisoner as instructed. He was captured approximately one hour after midnight. I trust he has the information Your Majesty desires."

It was a formal report, you understand. That was how one spoke to the Emperor on parade.

Napoleon took a step forward. He looked me up and down with that quick flicker of the eyes which told him more about a man in two seconds than most of us learn about our best friends in a lifetime. Then he turned to my prisoner.

The little Austrian officer was a trifle in advance of

me, and I stole a look at his face. It was strangely white. The flush of rage had departed from it, and a look of interest had taken its place, and that was only natural. One does not meet Napoleon every day, and never without emotion.

Napoleon smiled. A curious expression flitted over his face, and he turned to me sharply.

" The name of your prisoner, Captain de Blanchegarde ? " he asked.

" I do not know his name, Sire," I answered. " The prisoner has a violent habit of speech, and I thought it well to — er — discourage conversation."

The Emperor was still smiling, and Lannes was smiling too. Then suddenly the face of Napoleon changed. He looked at me severely, and my heart sank like a stone within me.

" Captain de Blanchegarde," he said sternly, " I hoped you would bring me a man from the Corps of General Hiller. You have not done as I expected."

My heart was now a lump of ice in my breast. I made no excuse. The Emperor would never hear excuses.

Then suddenly, to my amazement, he moved towards me and pulled me by the ear. It was the famous gesture. He used it only when he was specially pleased with us. My spirits rose again. My blood was singing.

" No," said the Emperor, " you have brought me General Hiller himself."

Napoleon, still holding to my right ear, pulled me gently to and fro.

" Come, *Major* de Blanchegarde," he said, pulling a paper out of his pocket, and thrusting it into my hand. " You must be tired. Allow me to offer you breakfast. And perhaps General Hiller will join us. I promise not to ask him any questions he might consider indiscreet.

I think we know now the position of his corps. He is too good a general to be separated from his men. We breakfast in Mölk, *mon général*, and tonight we will dine in Vienna."

And that, of course, is the end. . . . The grenadiers ? . . . Yes, they got the Cross all right. Nor were old Fritz and his men forgotten. I took them the purse myself, thinking how useful it might have been to me.

What's that you say, Suzanne ? . . . Another story ? . . . Not tonight, my dear. What would our mother say ? Some other time perhaps.

The Poodle of the Princess Alberoni

§ 1

DID I ever tell you the story of Madame Entremont and the poodle of the Princess Alberoni? It was but a drawing-room affair, and I had, upon my word, forgotten it these forty years, and in so doing I was, as it happens, only obeying the orders of the Emperor himself — as you shall see. But there can be no harm in remembering it now.

It was your little *caniche*, Suzanne, who put me in mind of it. I have been amusing myself this afternoon watching him at his tricks. He is clever, your little *caniche*, and I see you have taught him a trick with a story to it if you did but know — I mean when he gives three barks for the Emperor and stands on his hind legs as stiffly as a grenadier of the Old Guard. But I do not think he will be of such good service to your Napoleon III as the poodle of Princess Alberoni was to his uncle.

• Yes, Gaston, you may put another log on the fire, and I will tell you about it. And you may also pour me out another glass of burgundy. That is the wine for a soldier, old or young — the only wine the Emperor ever drank, and '42 was an excellent year.

What is that, Suzanne? . . . You want to know what the poodle did for the great Napoleon. But that is the end of the story and not the beginning.

I was a Major in those days, and had just returned with the rest of the Army from the victorious campaign that ended in the battle of Wagram. You have often heard me tell you of that fight, and of how I was wounded at Znaim a few days later. Wagram, you remember, was where Masséna went into battle in a carriage, drawn by four horses, for he had been wounded, and could not bear the saddle. But that is another story.

In November 1809 I was appointed to the staff of the Prince of Essling. As aide-de-camp to the Prince you may imagine I had my entries everywhere in Paris, and Paris in December 1809 and the first months of 1810 was very gay. We had just returned from yet another brilliant campaign, and a large part of the Army had already been warned for service in Portugal and Spain. So we were making the most of the time between. Never have I seen Paris gayer than during that winter — banquets and balls every day, both at Court and in the private houses of the great men of the Empire. The Emperor had ordered his Marshals to be gay and he paid them to be lavish. He said it was good for trade and that it kept up the spirits of the nation. And that, it seems, was necessary, for, after the Berlin decrees, trade in France was not what it ought to have been.

Imagine, then, all the big people in Paris and those who pretended to be big, rivalling each other in the magnificence of their entertainments, and imagine your old grandfather, young in those days and without too much in his pocket, having the time of his life. Why, I hardly had to pay for a meal, and that was a consideration, let me tell you, when every franc had to be devoted to equipping oneself for the next campaign.

§ 2

Of all the entertainments, the most magnificent and popular were the fancy-dress balls given by the Princess

Alberoni. She was the wife of the Italian Ambassador. The Emperor, as you know, was King of Italy in those days and his stepson Eugène was reigning as Viceroy. The Prince Alberoni was thus accredited to Napoleon's Court as Ambassador of the Viceroy of Italy. He lived in a magnificent house in the Champs Élysées, at the corner of the Avenue Montaigne. The Princess, who was a charming woman, kept a number of dogs, poodles for the most part, which were then coming into fashion in our society, and she named them all after the Emperor's victories. The best of them was Marengo, a fine black dog with floppy ears and a very solemn expression, and his accomplishments included standing to attention whenever he heard the name Napoleon pronounced. There was nothing that dog could not do, and the Princess was devoted to him. He was, in fact, the apple of her eye, always carefully groomed and fed, and a special servant was detailed to look after him. He ran about just as he liked and was allowed to wander through any room in the great house quite freely. " Love me, love my dog." Everyone paid him marked attention, especially those persons frequenting the Princess Alberoni's *salon* who were a little doubtful of their invitations. And I verily believe the animal saw through it all. He was clever enough for that.

The Prince Alberoni, being only a civilian, was allowed to give these fancy-dress balls I have mentioned. The etiquette for officers of the Army was more severe. Such mummery did not become a Marshal of France, but there was no such restriction on a mere Ambassador ; and, as I say, the balls were popular, and no one, strangely enough, took more delight in them than the Emperor himself. He would often go to them incognito, accompanied only by Duroc, Grand Marshal of the Palace and Duke of Friuli, his closest friend. Usually they wore black dominoes and were heavily masked. The Emperor would move freely amongst the guests listening to their conversation and quizzing the ladies, of whom, needless to say, there were a large number. It was all the more amusing from his point of view, for most of the ladies unmasked fairly soon after their arrival at the ball, that is to say all the pretty ones did so : the others perhaps enjoyed themselves more by conforming strictly to the etiquette of the ball.

You will understand, of course, that these little escapades of the Emperor caused a certain amount of misgiving to Fouché, the Minister of Police, and that fairly elaborate precautions were taken. For example, the Prince Alberoni invariably submitted a list of all the guests he proposed to invite before the invitations were issued, and no card was sent to anyone of whom the police might disapprove. There were also a number of secret agents in the ballroom, suitably disguised of course, and a battalion of the Old Guard was on duty round the *Hôtel*. Each guest, moreover, was required to unmask as he presented his card of invitation at the door. It was, therefore, difficult to go to these balls uninvited, as I am told is the fashion amongst the unmannerly young people of today. Once past the door, however, the guests had no idea that they were under any form of supervision, for the police were very discreet in the ballroom.

§ 3

I received invitations to all these affairs as a matter of course in my capacity as aide-de-camp to the Prince of Essling. Some days before the last of these fancy-dress balls, which took place, if I remember rightly, late in

January 1810, I visited, with my mother, some old friends of ours, whom I will call Monsieur and Madame X, for as they were implicated only by pure accident in the affair, and as they have numerous relatives still alive, it would be indiscreet of me to give you their names. I forget who were present at the tea-drinking, but it was quite a large party. There were de Bourdigny, Dupont, Vezy and half a dozen others, all aides like myself, and a corresponding number of ladies, amongst whom was one who attracted universal attention.

You have heard, my children, of the Amazons. They were a mythical race of female warriors. The woman of whom I am speaking must have had one of them for an ancestor. She was almost as tall as myself, and I stood six feet four inches in those days. She was a great, strapping creature, all in proportion to her height. She was not what you would call beautiful and, alas! she would never see forty-five again. But she had lovely hair — blond and a great deal of it. Her gestures matched her figure. She spoke and moved like a dragoon.

Such was Madame Entremont, and I was soon to know a good deal more than I shall ever remember about her and her grievances, which were, as I discovered, as large as her person.

For, as bad luck would have it, she took a fancy to me — it did occasionally happen, my children, where ladies were concerned, and she poured into my ears an interminable story of her woes. She was a widow, it seemed, and the pension she drew as her husband's relict — he had been some sort of official in the Ministry of the Interior — was, according to her views, inadequate. She had repeatedly petitioned for redress, as she called it — in other words, she was asking that her pension should be doubled. That day she was especially indignant. For she had been refused, once and for all, an audience with the Emperor, to whom she wished the matter to be referred.

I did not argue with her. I just nodded from time to time and any normal person would have realised that I only nodded because I must. But Madame Entremont seemed to think that I had for her a genuine sympathy. Soon I grew tired of nodding and by way of a diversion I asked her whether she was going to the ball of the Princess Alberoni, which was to take place in a few days' time. That again was unfortunate. It seemed that she fully intended to go to the ball and had, in fact, boldly written to Princess Alberoni requesting an invitation on the ground that she was the widow of a public man. The Princess, in the kindness of her heart, had sent her a card, but, as I discovered later, had only done so at the last moment, so that the name of Madame Entremont did not appear on the list of guests submitted to the police. Otherwise she would certainly not have been admitted, being a *mauvais sujet*. She talked loudly of the ball and, when she discovered that I also was going, she even more loudly praised her own good fortune. We should be able, she said, to go the ball together. She knew but few people in Paris, and doubted whether she would find any friends among the Ambassador's guests.

" But now that I have so handsome an escort," said she, " my success at the ball will be assured."

I am merely repeating what she said, you understand, and I need hardly assure you that it filled me with dismay.

§ 4

It was two days later, I think, that I found myself on duty at the Tuileries. I had come to the Palace with

Masséna who was seeing the Emperor that morning about the new campaign in Portugal. Our armies in the Peninsula were not at that time doing as well as we had expected. We had, in fact, suffered more than one reverse at the hands of my Lord Wellesley. This Wellesley was, as perhaps you know, an English General — the one that was made a Duke shortly before his rescue by Blücher at Waterloo. It was now being proposed that we should send Masséna, the darling child of victory, to try a turn with the Englishman and effect the conquest of Portugal. I was lounging in one of the anterooms with several of the Emperor's aides. There were three or four of us, grouped in an embrasure of the window, and we were looking out on the new Rue de Rivoli, and playing " Beaver." It was a silly game but we all played it at the time. You just waited for the men as they passed and betted on " whiskers " or " no whiskers ". Whiskers, you know, were *de rigueur* in those days except for civilians, though Soult and Bernadotte wore none. I had just won two napoleons off Vezy, I remember, when we heard a commotion on the stairs outside, and the sound of a high-pitched voice, which for the moment I did not recognise. We turned as one man, and there before us was one of the Emperor's chamberlains evidently trying to prevent someone from entering the room. He had his face to the enemy, but was in full retreat, and almost at once the intruder appeared.

Imagine my dismay. The chamberlain was a small man and at that moment I wished devoutly I had not myself been quite so large and obvious. For the person behind him was my fair encounter of two days before. She was wearing a blue-velvet hat perched on the back of her head and a dress of yellow taffeta, cut low in the back and front, with long black gloves. She seemed about eight feet high, and with her yellow frock and her sallow skin, looked like one of those statues which the First Consul brought back from Egypt in '99. She was driving the wretched chamberlain before her, and whenever he paused, she placed a mighty hand on his chest. Her advance was irresistible. The poor man had no time to form square. The heavy cavalry was upon him, and when at last she steered him into a footstool, he fell flat on his back and left us face to face with his assailant.

She waved a white card in the air with an ample gesture.

" Where," she demanded, " is the Emperor ? "

For a moment we all stood silent in astonishment. Then I drew back a pace into the window. I seldom move into cover, but this was not an ordinary emergency. It was a fatal move, my children. Never flinch before the enemy. It is better to stand your ground, come what may. She saw me at once. She smiled. At least I think it was a smile.

" Major de Blanchegarde," she said, coming at me with her hand extended. " This is most fortunate. I have, as you see, permission to visit the Emperor. You will perhaps be good enough to conduct me to His Majesty."

She held out the white card as she spoke, the card which was issued from the office of Duroc to persons who have been granted an audience. I glanced hurriedly to left and right. Would you believe it, my children ? I was alone. Not a man in sight. The cowards. . . . Mechanically I put out my hand. She thrust the card into it. I glanced at it, then up at her where she stood tapping a gigantic heel on the blue carpet sewn with golden bees.

" Madame," I said, and I hoped that my voice was

firm, " this card is a month old."

" I am aware of that, Major de Blanchegarde," said she. " But it is not my fault if the Emperor is badly served. The card is a month old because His Majesty should have seen me a month ago."

" I am sorry, Madame," I said, " but I'm afraid I'm not in a position to be of any assistance to you. This is a matter for the personal aides-de-camp of His Majesty."

I looked savagely round as I spoke to the embrasure in which Vezy and his friends were presumably in ambush.

She took no notice of my observation, but, with a look that might have felled an ordinary man, she moved suddenly forward towards the door leading to the Emperor's private apartments.

Vezy, never so heroic as in that critical moment, sprang from his hiding-place, and the chamberlain, who had by now succeeded in getting to his feet, pattered after her. She was within three paces of the door, however, when it suddenly opened and Masséna appeared on the threshold. He was in uniform, looking graver than usual. He realised, none better, the responsibilities of the campaign in front of him. The Amazon halted a moment at the sight of him and then made as though to push him aside. His eyebrows went up and he beckoned me with a slight gesture.

" Who is this ? " he asked, with his strong accent of the Midi.

" It is Madame Entremont, Monseigneur," I answered hastily. " She wishes to see the Emperor."

" I *insist* on seeing the Emperor," she corrected, in no way abashed by the presence of a Marshal of France. She even thrust out her large hand, so that for a terrible moment I thought she was going to treat him as she had treated the chamberlain. Masséna drew back a pace — fortunately there was no stool ; then with a smile bowed to her courteously and stepped briskly to one side. Madame Entremont swept through the door, while the aides all stood aghast. Masséna, however, seemed quite unruffled and stood gently pulling at his grizzled moustache.

We had no time to wonder what would happen, for a moment later, there she stood again, in a whirlwind of yellow silk, glaring with hot eyes at the smiling Marshal.

" The Emperor is not there," she said. " What have you done with him ? "

Masséna bowed again.

" I'm sorry, Madame," he replied. " His Majesty has just left in his coach for Fontainebleau."

Through the open window, as he spoke, came the clatter of hoofs and the jingle of harness, followed, a moment later, by the sound of cheering in the streets.

Madame Entremont turned upon us in a fury.

" This time," she exclaimed, " he has escaped me. Next time he will be less successful."

She turned round abruptly and flounced from the room, not pausing to look again at any of us.

Vezy sighed with relief, and mopped his forehead. Masséna looked after her quietly, then, turning to us, tapped the side of his head with his forefinger.

" Poor creature," he murmured. " But I am glad the Emperor left by the other door. Who on earth let her in ? She might have proved . . . difficult."

§ 5

I set out for the Princess Alberoni's ball at about nine in the evening. I was in good spirits that day.

My preparations for the coming campaign were well advanced, and I had in particular been lucky enough to buy cheaply an admirable mare from Count Canisy who was in charge of the Emperor's stables. It was, therefore, with a light heart that I presented myself at the *Hôtel*.

The place was brilliantly lighted and surrounded, as I have already said, by a battalion of the Old Guard, in their blue-and-white uniforms and tall bearskins. All the guests were in fancy dress, but I had contented myself with wearing a blue-silk domino over my mess uniform. It is not fitting, I maintained and still do maintain, for soldiers on active service to dress themselves up like puppets or waxworks. Besides, the Emperor wore a domino, and there were many who followed his example.

I walked up the marble steps between a double row of lackeys in the livery of the Prince, green and silver. I was met at the door by the major-domo, to whom I handed my card of invitation, at the same time removing my mask for the benefit of two unobtrusive individuals who stood at the entrance disguised as Scottish chieftains. It is a curious dress, my children, and one which does not become the French. They wore short green skirts with lines running at right angles on them, and the bearskin, instead of being worn upon the head, was strung about the waist where it hung like an apron almost to the knees. They were two of Fouché's men and, knowing me well by sight, they let me pass immediately.

I moved slowly into the ballroom. Although I had come fairly early, the crush was already great. The room itself was magnificent, and lit by a large number of blown-glass chandeliers from Venice, containing

I

hundreds of wax candles, which in themselves sufficed to overheat the room. Seldom have I seen more magnificent costumes. Everyone was in silk or velvet, and many of the ladies carried great fans and wore headdresses of plumes.

I stood for a moment or two near the door, watching the dancers, for a quadrille was in progress. The orchestra was playing in a little musicians' gallery hidden by a fantastically designed mirror so that it appeared that the music came from the reflection — a pleasing conceit. It was, as I have said, a brilliant scene and, without a care in the world, I was promising to enjoy myself to the full.

But suddenly my doom was upon me. Among the dancers near the orchestra I became aware of a commotion as when a pike swims into a shoal of roach, and before I could quite make out the cause of it there came sailing through the midst of them a figure that could belong to only one person that I knew. She was wearing a simple robe of white calico, with a red corsage, the whole confection being covered with little bits of variegated ribbon. She was masked, of course, but I had no difficulty in recognising Madame Entremont. I have already told you of her hair. She had chosen this costume apparently to set it off, for she wore it in two long plaits reaching almost to the knees. Perched on the top of her head, at a rakish angle, was a little straw hat worn over one ear and secured by a large pin. The simplicity of this costume among the silk and velvet of the other guests and the great size of the creature wearing it attracted universal attention. By a most unfortunate mischance I had taken off my mask and was fanning myself with it when I first perceived her. I at once made to readjust it, but it was too late.

" It is Major de Blanchegarde," she said, and came at me like one of Nansouty's cuirassiers. Everyone looked in my direction and there was some tittering among the guests. I was red, as I knew, to the ears.

" I have at last a cavalier," she continued. " I have also a bad thirst. You shall lead me to the buffet."

I do not know how long it took us to get clear of the ballroom — years, it seemed to me. But at last we reached a buffet in a side room and I was then able to note that the thirst of Madame Entremont was proportionate to her voice and stature. She drank champagne as a charger drinks water at the end of a long march. My children, I swear it was an accident. Madame Entremont was six feet four ; she was dressed to provoke attention ; she had made of me the most conspicuous man in all that assembly. But even so I did not wilfully abandon her. No, not though she went so far as to propose that we should return to the ballroom and waltz together. As I fell into step beside her, I knew well what was in store, but I was prepared to face it.

Relief, however, came from an unexpected quarter. I had bowed formally to Madame Entremont and we had moved as far as the entrance to the ballroom, when I saw a number of men dressed as pages of the time of Henry IV moving rapidly round the room. I recognised them immediately. They were the secretaries of Prince Alberoni.

" The Prince requests all his guests to put on their masks," they were saying. " The Emperor is at hand."

I bowed again to Madame Entremont.

" I am sorry," I said. " I left my mask on a table near the buffet. I beg you to excuse me for just one moment."

I hastily returned to the buffet, found my mask and — less hastily, perhaps, made my way back to the ball-room. Madame Entremont was not, however, where I had left her. I will not say that I looked for her with diligence. I will not swear that I even entered the ball-room. I had, you understand, no wish to dance. I accordingly climbed the broad staircase with its bronze balustrade to the first floor and entered the gaming rooms. Play was running high, and alas! I could not afford to lose a franc at that stage of my career. So, being the sort of man that can resist anything except temptation, I wandered away from the tables and retired to a little *salon*, half in darkness, where there was but a single alabaster lamp on the table. There I sank into a comfortable chair and pulled off my mask. A passing footman brought me an excellent *sorbet*. It was not the evening I had anticipated, but my partner had deserted me and I had no desire to be intrusive. Soon, perhaps, I would go down again and, if she was no longer there, console myself with another and smaller partner. Meanwhile I would rest in this pleasant corner.

I had not been there more than a few minutes, how-ever, when two men, rather short and wearing black dominoes and black masks, entered the little *salon*.

" We can avoid the crowd here," said one of them.

Then, noticing me, he beckoned and called to me imperiously by name. I could not see who it was, the man being masked, but there were few men who would have ventured to summon me in that way. I rose and moved towards him.

" I am Duroc," he said at once. " This is the Emperor."

He indicated the second masked man with a slight gesture of his right hand.

" His Majesty," he continued, " is tired and somewhat overcome by the heat. He wishes to rest a moment
here. You will, therefore, remain with me near the door
and keep off anyone who may happen to enter."

I bowed and said nothing.

The Emperor crossed the room, laying his hand on
my shoulder as he passed.

" It is very hot," he said, as he sat down in an armchair in one of the angles of the room. The Emperor,
as I think I have told you, was a brilliant conversation-
alist.

Duroc and myself took up two other chairs and
arranged them so as to screen the Emperor as far as
possible. We then sat down facing the doorway. Duroc
kept his mask, but conversed freely with me as though
we had been old comrades. We talked about the last
campaign and he referred, incidentally, to my famous
exploit at Mölk and to the Emperor's pleasure that so
gallant a soldier had survived. Of course I am only
telling you what he said.

Presently Napoleon called out. I turned round, but
Duroc was instantly at his side.

" You have the handkerchiefs ? " said the Emperor.

" Here, Sire," answered Duroc, and he produced two
white silk handkerchiefs, with which the Emperor wiped
his face and neck. Then he turned to me.

" De Blanchegarde," he said, " be good enough to
get me a large glass of iced water."

I bowed and sped from the room. The slightest
service to the Emperor, you understand, was an honour.
I thought it best to go to the buffet downstairs, since I
did not know my way about the Palace, and did not want
to keep the Emperor waiting. I accordingly went
straight to the room to which I had previously conducted

Madame Entremont, where I obtained the water. Two men approached me as I was leaving the *salon*. They were the two members of the secret police whom I had seen before at the door in the curious costume of the Scots.

One of them whispered in my ear as I passed :

" Is Major de Blanchegarde prepared to guarantee the purity of the water he is carrying in that tumbler ? "

" I think so," I answered. " I took it from one of the many *carafes* standing on that table over there."

The men nodded and passed on.

Yes, my children, the Emperor was well guarded — it was indeed very necessary to be careful.

The Emperor received the water with such pleasure that I thought he must be very thirsty. To my surprise, however, he drank only a small mouthful and then, wetting the handkerchiefs one by one in the iced water, he asked me to put one of them on the nape of his neck, while he himself took the other and placed it on his face. When we had done this he repeated several times : " That is good . . . that is good."

At a sign from Duroc I returned to my post by the door. I had hardly reached it, however, when I heard a heavy rustle of draperies and there, suddenly on the threshold, stood Madame Entremont.

For a moment we were motionless, neither of us speaking. The Emperor had hastily pressed the handkerchief over his face so that it completely covered it.

" At last, Monsieur," she exclaimed.

" Madame," I said quickly, in order that there should be no misunderstanding, " I was beginning to fear that you had abandoned me."

From the corner of my eye I could see Duroc, beside

the Emperor in the shadow, signalling me to take the lady away.

" I do not abandon my friends," she said in that great voice of hers.

" Indeed," I said. " Then perhaps I may claim the dance for which I was hoping." I hoped the Emperor would realise the extent of my devotion.

" It is suffocating," she replied. " Let us rather rest here a moment. The night is still young. You shall have your dance, Major de Blanchegarde."

So saying, she descended upon the chair left vacant by Duroc who was standing by the Emperor, and beckoned me imperiously to seat myself at her side. What could I do ? It was no use Duroc doing his signalling exercises in the corner. While Madame Entremont sat there, completely blocking the only exit from the *salon*, the Emperor, whom she was so anxious to see, was virtually a prisoner. I sat down with the best grace I could.

She leaned towards me, nodding her large head with its absurd hat, secured by what I now perceived to be an Italian stiletto of very slender workmanship, scarcely larger, in fact, than a hatpin.

" I am waiting for *him*," she said.

My heart stood still.

" He is sure to be at the ball," she went on. " He always comes to these parties. All the world knows it. He has no manners at all, the little Corsican, and is glad of a chance to be free of the etiquette which he imposes on us all. I shall see him tonight, and at last I shall have justice."

I looked at her in dismay, remembering the comment of Masséna. Her eyes were bright and had a glassy look. Her fingers were twitching on the fan she carried. The poor creature was obviously crazy with her grievances — and, not to put too fine a point on it, my children, she had visited, more than once I am afraid, the buffet to which I had introduced her earlier in the evening. Brandy, it seemed, on top of all that champagne. I waved my handkerchief in the air.

" Justice," I echoed, completely at a loss. " The Emperor is always just."

" He has twice refused to see me," she continued. " Either he shall give me satisfaction tonight or he shall pay the penalty. I have waited long enough. I shall ask once again for redress. He will again refuse. He has the obstinacy of a pig — this Bonaparte."

I liked this less than ever. For one thing, it was distinctly compromising. The Emperor must be wondering what sort of company I was in the habit of keeping.

" Madame," I said, " you do not know me well — scarcely at all in fact — or you would know that you are talking to a loyal subject of the Emperor. I beg you to control yourself."

For a moment she did not answer, but just sat there glaring balefully at me. She had an expression in her eyes which would have daunted a basilisk. Out of the corner of my eye I could see Duroc still frantically signalling. Once more in desperation I sought to induce her to return to the ballroom.

" Madame," I said, " I can assure you you will do no good by violence. Let us return to the ballroom and if, as you think, His Majesty will see fit to honour Prince Alberoni by his presence here tonight, you will be more likely to find him watching the dancers than you will be if you remain here."

For a moment she hesitated, glaring at me. Then

she got suddenly to her feet. Her movement reminded me of a charger I once had, an obstinate devil of a horse, that put his off foot into an icy puddle on the field of Austerlitz, and falling, flung me over his head. The fact that I landed in a bush saved me from death or injury, and I remember watching from its depths while I was trying to tear myself loose, his rolling eye and his convulsive struggles to get to his feet again. Madame Entremont's movements in that little room brought back vividly to me the great, thrashing hooves and whirling legs of my charger. Her large, ungainly gestures were in the end successful and at last she stood, planted upon her huge feet. Needless to say I had risen during her struggles and was holding out my arm. In a moment the situation would have been saved. In a moment I would have had her through the door, moving towards the ballroom, where I should undoubtedly have contrived to tip the wink to one of Fouché's men and then all would have been well.

At that very instant, however, fate in the shape of the Princess Alberoni's fine black poodle intervened. Marengo — you will remember that was his name — chose the precise instant when I was escorting my unwieldy partner to the door to make his entrance. He trotted towards us, his head held high, his fine-bred nostrils twitching. My partner held out an enormous hand with evident intention of bestowing upon him an elephantine caress. Marengo, however, was evidently in no mood for this kind of attention. He avoided her neatly and then continued on his way across the room till he reached the semi-recumbent form of the Emperor.

Even then all might have been well had not Madame Entremont, seemingly incensed by the indifference of the dog to her advances, swung ponderously round and addressed him in stentorian tones as her " little spoilt cabbage ". At the very instant that this grotesque reproach passed her lips, Marengo had reared himself up and placed his front paws on the Emperor's white breeches. Seeing this movement Duroc chose, inadvisedly enough, to interfere. He bent forward to induce the animal to assume a more seemly position and not to disturb His Majesty, but at the same instant Napoleon, aroused by the touch of the dog, sat up and his shoulder struck lightly against Duroc's outstretched hand. The shock could scarcely have been felt by either of them, but it was enough. The wet handkerchief fell from the Emperor's face. My tremendous companion halted dead in her tracks, so abruptly that I stumbled. Recovering myself in an instant I essayed to lead her on, murmuring something to the effect that we should be late for the next dance.

I might just as well have tried to move the Pyramid in front of which the Emperor gained one of his notable victories, or uproot the *doyen* of the oaks in the forest of Fontainebleau. She was immovable. She was as the Rock of Ages. I was helpless. Desperately I stared in the same direction as her gaze. As I feared, it was fixed full on the Emperor. At that instant she came to life.

She moved, my children, and she moved with the weight and swiftness of the wild elephant, but the direction she took was not through the door but back into the room.

" *Napoléon !* " she shouted, and at the same instant dragged herself loose from my restraining hand.

" *Napoléon !* " she shouted again, and took two steps forward. Her eyes were glassy and there was a faint suggestion of foam on her lips. At that instant I knew she was mad and that the Emperor was in mortal danger.

As I flung myself desperately in her path I saw her huge right hand move to the ridiculous hat she was wearing on top of her long yellow locks and pluck from it, horror of horrors, the pin shaped as a stiletto.

Desperately I sought to grapple with her, but before I could obtain any kind of grip, her other huge hand had planted itself full upon my chest. She gave one thrust and I was served as the luckless chamberlain had been served at the moment of our first encounter. My children, it was like the kick of a mule. I staggered back and, as ill luck would have it, one of those occasional stools that are so seldom equal to the occasion took me at the back of the knees and I fell heavily on to the carpet. For a moment I knew utter panic. There was this wild fury moving straight to the Emperor, who was now on his feet, and there was no one but Duroc to stay her wild course.

" *Napoléon !* " she shouted a third time.

No one to withstand her ? I was wrong. There was one person in the room, one person who at the sound of the beloved Emperor's name had risen and stood stiffly to attention. Full in her path was Marengo, the black poodle of the Princess. At the sound of the sacred name he had sat up on his haunches, his forelegs held stiffly out in front of him as though grasping an invisible musket at the present. He made a fine sight, but Madame Entremont did not see it. She had eyes only for her objective, the Emperor. She swept forward one pace, two paces. At the third she encountered Marengo. It was a fine shock. No soldier of the Old Guard could have stood more firmly in the presence of charging cavalry than did that noble specimen of canine courage. He did not budge an inch. One of Madame Entremont's huge feet went one side of him, the other the other, so that the dog was caught in the swell of her long skirt. She tripped and stumbled, snatching at her skirt with one hand, but still holding the stiletto in the other.

I had by this time got free of the confounded stool onto which she had pushed me. I scrambled to my feet, my face burning from the insult I had received. I sprang forward and laid hold of her, just as Duroc, his face grown suddenly white behind the mask, thrust himself in front of the Emperor.

The colossus in my arm swayed like a tree in the wind. I hung on to her doggedly, though my arms were almost torn from their sockets. It was as much as I could do to hold her. I could certainly never have mastered her.

Reinforcements, however, were at hand. There was a shrill barking on my right flank. Marengo was coming into action. The dog leapt at her and, seizing a piece of her skirt in his teeth, thrust out his four legs into the thick carpet and stood firm. Something was bound to give way. There was a rending sound, and a large section of the white calico skirt parted from the red corsage. The gallant poodle wasted no time worrying his trophy but sprang again at such of the skirt as remained. There was another sound of tearing.

Madame Entremont's extravagant costume was in ruins ; in a moment she would be standing in her shift. She gave a howl of fury and, twisting round in my arms, she dealt me a savage blow with the stiletto. I bear the mark to this day, a little scar high up on the right shoulder. Her face as she turned upon me was terrible to behold. Her mask had slipped and her bloodshot eyes glared balefully into mine. Tears of rage drove furrows through the rouge and powder on her cheeks. It was the face of a maniac.

The struggle did not last more than a moment. Strong hands had gripped her and she was borne backwards. The two police *agents* dressed as Scots had appeared and, aided by another of their kidney, in the guise of a Roman Centurion, they had her on the floor and in a trice had bound her wrists and ankles with the strips of her own skirt, lying in shreds on the carpet.

Marengo was delighted with these proceedings and scampered round the struggling group barking loudly and wagging his tail as in the manner of successful dogs. I believe he knew very well what he had done. Many have received the Cross for less.

The Emperor had not stirred. Silently he watched the *agents* of the police as they secured and gagged his assailant. At last, however, he stepped forward.

"Duroc," he said, "this lady has fainted. See that she is carried out without exciting the attention of the other guests. And remember, all of you, when you leave this room, the incident is forgotten."

"You hear that?" said Duroc to the *agents*. "The people of France would tremble if they should learn how near to death His Majesty had been."

The *agents* withdrew with their burden.

The Emperor turned to Duroc with a smile.

"You are wrong, Duroc," he said. "The people of France would not tremble. They would laugh. They laugh at everything — these Frenchmen, — but they do not laugh at me. That is the secret of my power. No one has yet laughed at Napoleon."

There was a movement behind us and we all three looked round.

The inevitable had happened. At the word "Napoleon" Marengo, whom we had for the moment forgotten, had come to attention. He was standing stiffly upon his hind legs, his bright eyes fixed expectantly on the Emperor.

The Emperor considered him a moment, then broke into one of his rare winning smiles. He took a step forward, stooped and took the little creature by the ear.

You know the gesture, my children. The Emperor had taken me by the ear on one or two occasions, but it had happened to other men. Marengo, so far as I know, was the only member of his species to be thus distinguished. His small body quivered with loyalty and pride.

The Emperor then drew himself up. Marengo, dropping to his forelegs, looked briskly about him.

" Major de Blanchegarde " — it was the Emperor speaking — " you will report to me at ten o'clock tomorrow morning at the Tuileries."

" At ten, Sire," said I.

The heavy blue-velvet curtains fell together over the door. I was alone with Marengo, who was looking at me, I swear, with intelligent commiseration. Happily, however, he had less cause to pity me than we either of us imagined. For the Emperor had no thought of scolding me for my part in the affair. He had, on the contrary, a mission for me to perform, which was to buy Marengo from his mistress as a gift for the new Empress Marie Louise, whom he married some months later. Needless to say, the Emperor's request was granted, and Marengo afterwards became a great favourite with the little King of Rome.

Madame Entremont ? . . . Alas, poor lady, she died about a year later, hopelessly insane, in the great hospital of the Salpêtrière.

THE END

PRINTED BY R. & R. CLARK, LIMITED, EDINBURGH